OFFERING HIS ARM

THE BRIDES OF PURPLE HEART RANCH BOOK 3

SHANAE JOHNSON

THOSE JOHNSON GIRLS

Edited by Alyssa Breck

Manufactured in the United States of America
First Edition November 2018

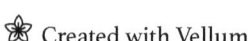 Created with Vellum

CHAPTER ONE

"That makes no logical sense."

Typically, when Reed Cannon said those words they were out of frustration as he tried to use facts and figures to prove what was clearly rational. Not this time.

Reed found himself running the fingers of his right hand through his hair. His lips split into a grin. His shoulders relaxed as he leaned back and looked at the screen.

"Not everything has to make sense, Specialist Cannon," said the woman on the other end of the voice only call.

She was wrong again. But Reed didn't mind. He liked the sound of her voice and was happy to hear her speak more words. Even if they were groundless and implausible.

"Some things you just know," she continued.

She had him. Because this was something that Reed, somehow, someway, just knew. Sarai Austin, the owner of the sultry voice that was heating up Reed's speakers, made sense. She was the proverbial One that the love stories told of.

The two of them had so much in common from their educational backgrounds; where he had studied Computer Science, she had studied Web Design. To their tastes in food; she detested Brussel's sprouts and you couldn't get him near a stalk of cruciferous poison. And then there was the most important commonality; they rolled in the same science fiction television and film fandoms.

"The Weeping Angels would totally and entirely decimate The Silence," Reed insisted, championing the scary statue villains in the hit science fiction television show *Doctor Who*.

"Nah unh," Sarai disagreed. "The way a Weeping Angel kills is when their victim looks away. That's when the stone figure comes alive, uncovers their eyes, and moves closer. If an Angel looks away from a Silence they'd forget they'd even saw them. Hence, the Silence would win."

"Sarai, you are so wrong."

"Oh, really, Reed? You may have gotten me on the Kirk over Picard argument. I still don't concede on the Spike was better for Buffy than Angel debate. But I'm right on this one."

"The Angel would turn back to stone as soon as the Silent looked at it. But the Angel can still see the Silent while it's a statue, so it wouldn't forget. Then, the moment the Silent blinks, the Angel would move in and kill it."

Sarai sighed on the other end of the line. Reed was getting used to that sound. It wasn't a sound of resignation. No, Sarai didn't give up so easily. She was about to move in for the kill, and Reed couldn't wait to hear her rebuttal.

"Ah, but that's where you're wrong. If they looked at each other, they'd be locked in a staring contest forever."

"You know this is a nonsensical argument about fictional characters?"

"I know that when you no longer have a leg to stand on in a debate you call it nonsensical."

Reed chuckled. Just as he was learning her quirks and idiosyncrasies, she was learning his. The sound of her light laughter surrounded him in stereo, but the box on the screen where the video of her face would be was dark. He wanted it to light up with the technicolor of a movie screen.

Reed and Sarai had been in communication for weeks on the dating app. Unlike many of the sites out there that had users swiping left or right depending on someone's attractiveness, this app was designed by sociologists, behavior scientists, and psychologists. The app matched users on levels of compatibility.

Sarai and Reed had earned a 98% compatibility score.

They'd gone through the seven stages of chatting via messenger. Then recently moved onto chatting over the voice feature of the app. It took four conversations to unlock the video feature. This was their fifth conversation.

The video feature's red button had changed to green with their last conversation, but neither of them had engaged it. They had no idea what the other looked like.

Reed wasn't fooled enough to say it didn't matter. He knew it did. The last three women he'd chatted with had balked when they'd seen what had become of his left arm. If he were honest, he'd admit that he'd rushed those relationships. Eager to get to the big reveal to see if they'd accept him.

He'd seen their rejection the moment the video went live. Two of them had tried to play it off that his prosthetic arm wasn't a big deal. One had ended the call immediately. Those other two never called back after their play acting.

Reed had taken things slow with Sarai. Mainly because of their high compatibility score. But also, because he liked chatting with her. Now they were outside a chat room and talking. But he couldn't delay it any longer. She had to see him. He just hoped that she accepted what came up on the screen.

"Sarai, you know what would make sense right now?"

"What? That the Cybermen could take out Daleks?"

Reed chuckled at the absurd idea, but he kept the conversation on track. "The video feature is available. Do you think maybe it's time we both went live on screen?"

The pause that ensued was deafening. Reed leaned back in his office chair. His office consisted of a desk shoved into the corner of the dining room he shared with no one. Reed wanted to share his dining room. He wanted to share his life. He felt certain that this was the woman who should be sitting next to him in this empty room.

"Why?" Sarai asked. Her voice was so tiny and small. So unlike the big personality that came through her text messages and voiced arguments.

"There's something about me that I think you should know. You have to see me in order to do that."

"Is this about your arm?" she asked. There was a note of relief in her voice. "You wrote that you have a prosthetic clear as day on your profile. It doesn't bother me."

"Women have said that to me in the past. Then when they see it, they sing another tune."

Reed leaned forward, getting closer to the dark video dot at the top of his screen, even though Sarai couldn't see him. "I really like you, Sarai. I'd like to take our relationship to the next level. A level where there are pictures. Unless ... you're not interested in going any further."

"No, no. It's not that. It's just ..."

Reed pulled close to the speakers listening intently as she inhaled. Still no resignation in her breath. She wasn't giving up. She was going to launch into another argument.

And he was going to give in. If she didn't want to see him live, or if she wanted to wait longer, he'd let her have her way. It didn't make sense, but something told him he'd have to be patient with this woman.

"All right. We can turn the cameras on."

Reed's heart pounded against his chest. He felt an itch in the palm of his hand. The itch was in the palm of his left hand which was no longer a part of his body. Phantom feelings came to him from time to time. Right now, the phantom fingers of his left hand wanted to reach out and click the button to turn on the feed that would finally bring him closer to meet his match. He reached out his right hand and flipped the switch.

CHAPTER TWO

*T*he green button flashed at Sarai, daring her to click it and show all of her imperfections to Reed. Sarai had used many dating apps over the last couple of years. This was usually the time that she typically closed her laptop and ran.

Well, not physically run. More metaphorically. Because Sarai Austin was in no shape to run. At least not any longer.

Just three years ago she'd strutted her stuff on some of the hottest runways in the world. Now, she rarely left the house or got out of her pajamas. Her life was spent entirely online, from keeping up with her various makeover blogs, to chiming in on fandoms, to socializing on various platforms with virtual friends. She'd gone to college online, earning a degree in web design, which came in handy with her current line of work.

She'd even had a couple of virtual boyfriends. Sarai was always careful to choose men who lived far enough away from her that it would make a weekend getaway cost-prohibitive. Her last relationship was with a guy in Russia. But he'd gotten tired of their chat room talks and unfriended her. The guy after that, he'd lived in Australia. When he'd wanted to FaceTime her, she'd ended the relationship.

What other choice did she have? She wasn't about to turn on the live feed so that they could see that her profile picture was three years old and thirty pounds lighter than she was in the present day. No, she didn't need that kind of rejection. She'd had enough from the modeling world.

So why was her finger hovered over the accept button to engage her video camera with Reed?

Because she looked forward to their chats every night. Because he made her laugh, genuinely laugh. And he made her think, and stretch her mind when she went toe to toe with him in one of their debates.

Also because he had no idea what she looked like, neither in the past nor in the present.

Sarai had made her way around nearly every

dating app out there. They all required a photograph as part of the profile. But not this one.

Instead, it engaged its users on a final exam about their life, asking questions about every facet of their being then matching potential couples based on an algorithm. Most of the guys Sarai had been matched with had been slightly over fifty percent. But she and Reed were a near perfect match at ninety-eight percent.

Maybe ... Just, maybe?

The computer screen blinked. The dark square that had been black filled with the face of a man. A handsome man. Sarai leaned in and wiped her monitor just to make sure all that perfection was real.

There were no wayward smudges on her lens. Reed Cannon was the stuff of a girl's dreams. He was handsome with his sandy blond hair and evenly tanned skin. His intelligent, dark eyes pierced her through the colored monitor. His lips were stretched in a cupid's bow that aimed straight for her heart. He looked like a young Luke Skywalker. All he needed was the lightsaber.

And he wanted to date her. So there had to be something wrong with him. She just couldn't figure it out.

Then she saw it; his prosthetic arm. He thought that would deter a woman? If anything it clenched the comparison to the young Jedi in her mind. What fan of the Star Wars franchise wouldn't find the loss of a limb in combat just a little hot?

"Sarai? Are you there?"

"Just a second."

Sarai took a deep breath. She could do this. She wanted to do this. She wanted to continue her conversations with Reed. And if they had to happen on screen, then so be it. She reached to click the mouse.

But before she did, she readjusted the camera to ensure that it only showed her from the shoulders up. All the weight she'd gained was in her belly and hips. She had a good collarbone. And the angles of her face were still attractive.

She'd made up her face, of course. What woman didn't immediately put on makeup after rolling out of bed in the morning whether they were receiving company or not? She wasn't a complete sloth.

She'd penciled in a smoky eye to accentuate the lift of her lids. She'd learned to kohl her eyes back in middle school under the tutelage of her Persian mother. As always, Sarai added some golden sparkles to bring out the hazel flecks in her green eyes.

Her lips were Autumn Red, a shade that highlighted the hints of red in her skin coloring. She'd kept her blonde hair up in an intricate knot that looked effortless, but she'd taken forty-five minutes to sculpt it. Her blonde tresses and green eyes were the only physical traits she'd gotten from her dad's side of the family. Everything else spoke to her Middle Eastern roots. All bundled up together, it made her look unique.

Well, it made her face look unique.

Checking once again to be sure that the virtual connection between her and Reed was disconnected, Sarai stood. She readjusted her shirt. The scoop neck flattered her collarbone making her look slimmer, but when she stood the shirt rode up exposing the rolls of her belly.

Her flesh wasn't on display. She'd double-Spanxed herself into the top. But that hadn't stopped the bubbles of her belly from rising up beyond the spandex. And the double-Spanx always made laughing, and talking, and breathing tricky. But beauty was pain, right?

Looking into the monitor, Sarai saw herself framed for the view. From the neck up, she had no trouble admitting she was a beauty. Once upon a time, her face had gotten her booked into the high end of fashion. It was just the rest of her that was a fat mess.

Her boobs, which had always been large, now had an equal amount of flesh under her armpits. Her arms now had an extra layer of fat that wiggled when she raised them. Her belly jiggled when she walked as if she were doing some belly dance from her ancestral homeland. And don't get her started on her thighs. She was sure Thor trembled when she walked.

Sarai took a deep breath. In her mind, she took those negatives statements and picked them apart. She was not the number on the scale. She was not solely what she saw reflected back in the mirror. The positivity technique she'd practiced in therapy helped to calm her nerves. But it didn't change her mind. Therapy had helped her cope, but it hadn't cured her. She would never be truly cured.

"Sarai? Has our connection gone bad?"

Sarai closed her eyes. She didn't want the connection she had with this man to break. But to keep it intact, she'd have to reach out and grab the other end of the knot.

Sarai clicked the button.

On the other end of the connection, Reed blinked a couple of times. Sarai chewed her lip as she waited for his verdict. Were her arms in the shot? Could he see the flab? Oh no, she hadn't contoured her cheekbones to perfection. Surely she looked like a chipmunk with a store of winter's nuts in her jowls.

"Wow," Reed whispered.

Sarai's hand shot to her cheek. Was it that bad? What had she been thinking? She reached for the mouse to turn off the camera. The fat wobbled at the backside of her bicep as she did so.

"You're beautiful." Reed's smile stretched across his face. His dark eyes were crystal clear as he gazed at his screen. He didn't look disgusted. He looked pleased.

Maybe the camera subtracted a few pounds? There was the whole compression thing that happened as information traveled across the ether. He'd called her beautiful. It was nice to hear. But still, Sarai had a hard time believing it was the truth.

"*You're* beautiful," she parroted. Those words she believed. Reed could've easily broken into the modeling world with his looks.

"Not without all my parts." He held up his prosthetic arm.

"Nonsense." Sarai barely gave it a glance. She

was more intent on the light in his eyes as he looked at her in the monitor. For the first time in a long time, she didn't mind her own reflection. "Put on a black glove, put a lightsaber in it, and I'll probably swoon."

Reed threw his head back and laughed. Sarai had loved eliciting laughter from him over the voice calls. Watching it happen in real time and in color was the most beautiful thing she'd ever seen. Suddenly, she couldn't remember why she'd waited so long to get to this step? If this was the sight she'd see at the top of the mountain, then she'd happily climb to get here.

"I know the protocol says to have four video chats before meeting in person," said Reed. "But I'd love to take you out to dinner."

Sarai felt herself falling off the high mountain at the mere thought. Dinner and date; two of the most feared words in her vocabulary. Reed wanted to not only see her in the flesh, he also wanted to watch her feed the excess amount of flesh on her person.

No, this wouldn't do.

Her hand reached for the disconnect button. Her index finger pointed at the END button on the screen. But she couldn't do it. She didn't want to lose the sight of his face. Or the twinkle in his eye as he looked at her. But neither could she see him in person the way she was.

"Come out with me, Sarai."

"I can't."

Reed's face fell. The light in his eyes dimmed. "Why not?"

"Because ..." Sarai looked out the window at the Montana skyline. One of the compatibility points was proximity. She knew Reed lived in the same state as her. He was only thirty minutes away. "Because I'm headed out of town. Out of the country, actually. I'll be in Paris for a couple of weeks doing makeup for my friend's photo shoot."

"A couple of weeks?" He looked devastated.

"But maybe we can see each other when I get back? That is if you're still interested."

"*If* I'm still interested?" He raised a brow and then leaned into the camera. "Would a Weeping Angel mute a Silent?"

Surprised laughter spilled out of Sarai. "Wait, we haven't come to an agreement on that."

"Then I suppose we'll have to keep debating it and settle it when we meet in person."

Reed's grin was contagious. Sarai found herself matching it, no longer concerned if her cheeks were puffing out. She had a plan.

There were plenty of weight loss programs that touted drastic changes in just thirty days. She'd start one tomorrow, and then, next month, she'd settle this fictional argument in real life with this man straight out of her dreams.

CHAPTER THREE

"How in the world did coffee spill inside the tower?" Reed crouched over the soggy computer terminal atop Dr. Patel's desk. The smell of fried wires and dark roast hit his nose.

Beside him, Soldier gave the wet ground a sniff. The little Chihuahua had been Reed's shadow for the last few weeks. His literal shadow as the small dog sported only three limbs like his human companion.

"Everything was going fine," said Dr. Patel. "And then the coffee holder suddenly retracted."

"Coffee holder?" Reed looked around the edge of the desk. There was no coffee holder. He knew that for a fact.

The interior design and functionality inside the

medical suite had been his responsibility. That had
included ordering the furniture and putting things
together. It would be a feat for a one-armed man, but
Reed was up for the task. He knew the job would
take multiple days so he'd ordered the computer
hardware and the office furniture to come in on
separate days.

But somehow the computers and office furniture
had all arrived on the same day. He was sure one of
his fellow soldiers had interfered with his order, or
simply held up the packages until they were all here
at the same time. That way Reed couldn't refuse
their help in putting things together when
everything came at once.

Xavier and Sean had set about screwing in and
hammering at the office furniture while Reed had
focused all of his attention on the computers. When
it came to computers, the other two men were pretty
useless.

Reed couldn't stand being useless. Or worse,
having someone think he was useless. Just because
he'd lost a limb didn't mean he'd lost out on life. He
still did all the things he loved.

He played video games. He played tabletop
games. He played sports. He dated.

Nope. Not having his arm wasn't holding him

back in the slightest. What was standing in his way, at the moment, was just an ocean.

The Atlantic Ocean stood between him and Sarai. That body of water was keeping Reed from achieving his goal of meeting her, courting her, wooing her, proposing to her, and then marrying her all within six weeks' time. Six weeks was the deadline for when the land the ranch sat on would change its zoning so that only families could live there daily. If Reed wanted to stay in this place where he was accepted, this place where he was useful, this place that had given him and his fellow soldiers a new purpose after exacting a pound of flesh from each and every one of them, then he'd have to get married.

That was why he'd been on the dating apps. He was looking for a bride who'd be compatible for him. If he could get the right woman to say yes in time, then he could stay for the rest of his life.

"Where exactly did you put your coffee cup, Dr. Patel?" Reed turned back to a problem he could solve.

He'd been a technology specialist in the armed forces. He was still able to perform all the tasks necessary to operate a computer. However, his disability status cut him out of a lot of the jobs he'd once been qualified for; namely those in combat zones. What was left for him were jobs he was overqualified for, jobs that didn't use 10% of his skillsets, jobs that would leave him bored to tears behind a desk all day long.

Reed turned to Dr. Patel as the older man pointed to the computer tower. Reed frowned. There was no coffee holder there.

Dr. Patel pressed a button. Soldier let out a stream of yips as a whirring sound emitted and the CD disk drawer opened. Both man and dog stared speechless at the dripping compartment meant for outdated circular disks. Then they both swiveled their heads to look up at the degreed man who sat in the office chair.

Last week, the psychologist had called Reed into his office. Dr. Patel had frowned at him insisting he'd called Reed for help with his computer problems ages ago. Reed was meticulous about appointments and being mindful of people's time. When he insisted he never got the message, Dr. Patel said he'd pressed the F1 button on his computer days ago. Reed had tried to explain that that particular HELP function wasn't connected to him.

Reed hadn't laughed at the older man. It was par for the course with the good doctor and technology.

When he'd first come to work at the ranch, Dr. Patel had asked Reed if he could reboot the internet because it was running slow that day.

"How is it you developed the dating app that has likely changed my life, but you have more trouble with technology than anyone I've ever met?" Reed asked as he sat down to work on the sopping wet terminal. He didn't have high hopes that the computer would survive. If it did survive this attack by the good doctor, its days were still numbered in this office.

"I didn't develop the app." Dr. Patel reached down and brought Soldier into his lap. The dog balanced on his hind legs as he stretched his small head up to receive scratches. "Only the compatibility questionnaire. That, I wrote out on paper. So, it's working well for you? You've found some matches."

"I found THE match. We're a 98% compatibility."

"That's wonderful. I'm so pleased to hear it. I suppose you'll be bringing her to the ranch soon? Possibly wedding bells in the near future?"

Reed hadn't told Sarai about the necessity for wedding bells yet. He hadn't told her he needed to get married in under two months if he wanted to keep his home and his livelihood here on the ranch.

He'd had enough rejection when he'd been discharged from the army.

"She's out of the country for a couple of weeks," said Reed. "But we've been talking every day for a while. Now we're video chatting and FaceTiming."

"Sounds like things are progressing. Pretty much like how I courted my wife. We wrote to each other and spoke over the phone before meeting face to face."

Dr. Patel had had an arranged marriage, and he'd been happily married for decades. He'd arranged many other people's marriages, including two other soldiers on the Purple Heart Ranch. Reed had thought about recruiting the doctor for his love life too, but he'd become gun-shy about meeting women in the flesh when he had some flesh of his own missing.

The app, which allowed two potential partners to get to know each other based on compatibility, was a much more palatable idea. And it had worked. He'd met Sarai who hadn't once balked at his lost limb.

"She's out of the country for weeks, you say?" asked Dr. Patel. "That'll be cutting it close. The zoning changes officially in just under two months."

"Yeah, I know." But Reed also knew that Sarai was it for him. He'd never met someone he'd had so much in common with. She was the one. He just knew it. "I guess I'll just have to get her to fall for me over the internet."

The computer before him sparked and whizzed. Reed jumped back toward safety. Soldier hopped down from Dr. Patel's lap and ran out of the room. The wires connecting the terminal to the router smoked. Looked like the terminal's number had come sooner rather than later.

CHAPTER FOUR

*S*weat dripped down Sarai's face as she pumped her arms and marched in time to the beat. Coordination was not her strong suit. Unless it had to do with accessorizing.

Her latest blog post had been on pairing the right bracelet with the right lip gloss and then moving day to night with the look. It had garnered her over a thousand likes in an hour. She was now a quarter hour into the new aerobic phase of her life and beads of sweat were her only companion.

Sarai's heart pounded as she tried to mimic the so-called easy movements of the skinny women in scant spandex on the screen. This workout promised it was simple enough for the very beginningist of beginners to succeed. So far she was succeeding, even if out of breath.

"Now, deep breath in," said the cheery leader on the screen.

The fitness expert's rock hard abs glistened with oil that made Sarai squint as she looked at the flat screen TV. Sarai looked away from the leader's example to the girl next to her. The carbon copy of the leader had been pointed out at the start of the video as the one to follow for a low-impact version of the exercises. Second fiddle's abs were cut and glistening too. Neither woman was breaking a sweat or grunting or grimacing like Sarai. Sarai couldn't help but wonder why no one on these videos looked like the people who pressed play at home?

It was no matter. The skinny leader had just told everyone to take a deep breath. That had to mean she was at the cool down portion of the workout. They'd stopped moving and were all taking deep, soothing breaths. Oh, thank goodness, it looked like it was over.

"And another deep inhale," said the workout leader. "Great job. You did it."

Sarai had done it. She'd made it through the entire workout. She was out of breath and a sweaty mess, but she'd done it.

"That completes the warm-up."

Sarai froze. Her arms had been stretched up in the inhale posture. Her head had been tilted up toward the ceiling, as though she were lost in a prayer of gratitude. Her head dropped down until she was looking square at the television screen to make sure she'd heard the skinny leader right.

Warm up?

That was the warm up?

Sarai dropped her arms to her sides. The flesh of her arms landed against the flesh of her love handles with a splat and a squish. She picked up the remote control and killed the power on the television set. The world turned to black, erasing the glistening abs of the trainers.

Thirty days. The cover on the DVD promised she'd lose up to twenty pounds in twenty days and become her best self. But Sarai couldn't make it twenty minutes in the program.

Outside, the beautiful Montana sky was darkening. She'd told Reed that she was out of town. It was the only reason she could think of to keep from seeing him in person while still seeing him virtually. Because she wasn't quite ready to give him up. She wasn't sure if she could ever give him up.

What was a guy like him doing on a dating site

anyway? He could have any girl he wanted with his looks and his intelligence and that smile. Oh, that smile.

Sure there was the reality of his missing limb. But Sarai forgot about it every time she spoke to him until he brought it up. Which he always did.

It was as though he wanted to shove it in her face. As though he wanted to make sure she caught it and that he wasn't hiding it. But it didn't matter to Sarai. So much about him outshined that one fault.

Unlike with her where there was so much of her to spread around. Sarai flopped down on the sofa. Her wide load displaced so much air that the magazines on the coffee table fluttered pages open. Spread in the center of the fold were girls she'd known in her modeling career. Their abs were even flatter than the fitness experts.

Models weren't meant to have a six-pack. Flat was better than bumps. For years, Sarai had striven to meet that imperfect ideal. But her body kept expanding in ways that were unacceptable to the powers that be in the industry.

The last straw had been when a casting director had ordered her to consume nothing but water the entire twenty-four hours before she was set to do a shoot. Sarai had done as she was told. She was welcomed onto the set the next day. The clothes hung off her frame in a way that showed her emaciated frame. And then, twenty minutes into the shoot, she collapsed.

That had been the last time she'd been on a set or walked a runway or even taken a selfie. She'd thought that had been her rock bottom when she'd hit the floor. She'd been wrong.

Her stomach grumbled at the memory. Or possibly from all the calories burned during that ten-minute warm-up of torture. Sarai hefted herself off the couch and went to the kitchen.

The contents of the fridge were a forest of green. Fresh, leafy greens. Green smoothies. Green tea. Her stomach grumbled again, this time in protest at the sight. No, that sound was her computer.

She had an incoming video call. She knew it couldn't be Reed. He believed she was in Paris, which would mean it was around two in the morning for her in France.

But this call was from France. The only people who'd be up in France at this time of night were the chic clique coming from a fashion show's after party.

Sarai shut the fridge and went over to her laptop.

She didn't bother framing the camera to only show her face. She flopped back in her office chair as her spandex let her rolls hang out.

"Hey, girl," Sarai said.

"Hey, girl," came a deep voice from across the web. A flash of light filled the dark frame, then a beautiful male face came into view.

Mason Lee had cheekbones that every woman would die for. His eyes were outlined in sparkling blue liner exaggerating the curve of his Asian features. His glossed lips were spread in a smile as he leaned in toward the camera as though he could peer into the screen.

"What are you wearing?" he asked.

"Spandex."

His bottom lip pushed up toward his top lip as though forming the top of a question mark. "Why?"

"I told you I was starting that exercise program today."

Mason's bottom lip pressed harder, curving even more. "Why?"

Sarai clucked her tongue at him, but his lips still remained in their curved question mark. She fluttered her hands up and down the tight fabric encasing and suffocating her body. "I'm finally trying to lose the weight."

"Sweetie, how many times do I have to tell you? Women pay to have the curves you have."

"Not in the modeling world, they don't."

"Well, you're not in this world any longer, are you?"

"Because I'm too fat."

Mason lips reformed their shape. There was no question this time. He was about to start a full-blown inquiry.

Sarai scrambled to correct her language. "It's just that time of the month. I'm not feeling like myself."

Her best friend didn't look convinced, but he did drop the crease between his brow. Sarai didn't need him to become concerned about her. She wasn't backpedaling into harmful behaviors. She was just having a bad day.

"You were always far too real to meet the unrealistic ideal of these idiots," Mason said.

"Says the man who models for a living."

"It's different for guys, and you know that. They want men with muscles and six-pack abs. They want women who look like little girls or little boys. You look like the full-grown woman you are. You are healthy, and your body functions exactly as it's meant to."

Sarai knew Mason was doing what BFFs did,

trying to make their bestie feel good about themselves. He also knew the things to say and what not to say to trigger her disorder. She wasn't triggered, just disappointed in her performance with the workout program.

"Well, you look like you worked up a sweat. How did it go?" he asked.

Sarai hung her head. "I didn't make it past the warm-up."

Now Mason's lips formed an O. But not one of surprise. It was a wince of commiseration. It hurt Sarai's brain just thinking about Mason's hours-long workout regimen.

"Wait a minute," he said. "Is this for that soldier?"

She twisted her lips instead of responding. Unfortunately, since the video was live her bestie saw the expression and read her correctly.

"Sarai, honey, you need to stop hiding behind your laptop. Just go and meet him."

For the first time in a long time, Sarai wanted to. She wanted to get dressed up and go out. She wanted to sit across from a man and feel all the jitters and excitement of a first date. She felt that every time she sat down with Reed at her laptop.

What would it feel like to sit across from him in real life?

"You've never talked about a guy this much before. And didn't you say he has no idea what you look like? That means he likes you for you."

"We video chatted the other day."

Mason squealed with delight. "Rai Rai, if this guy is as great as you say he is, he'll accept you for who you are, not what you look like."

Sarai chewed the inside of her lip, but she didn't answer. Her grumbling stomach filled the silence. She reached out to hit the mute button too late.

"What have you eaten today?" Mason asked, his lined eyes turned to inquisitive.

"I just finished working out. You're supposed to eat afterward."

Mason glared at her.

"The fridge is stocked with greens." Sarai's stomach grumbled again at the thought of the unappetizing green foods awaiting her.

"Sweetie, you have a habit of going to the extremes sometimes. I just don't want you to do that now."

"I'm good," Sarai said. "I'm not going down that path again."

Mason glared some more. "I worry about you when I'm not there."

Sarai and Mason had shared this townhouse for just under a year. But he was rarely at home with all of his bookings around the world. Sarai often forgot she had a roommate.

"I just don't want you falling back to old patterns," Mason was saying. "Maybe you should schedule some appointments with that doctor you used to see."

"Mace, I'm going to eat now. I don't need to see a shrink."

"Okay, okay." He held up his hands, but his lips were pressed up in that curved question mark again.

Sarai decided she'd rather cut the conversation short over going down the dark path of her past. "I'm gonna go eat, and you need to go get your beauty sleep."

"Sleep? Sweetie, I'm in Paris. This city never sleeps. We're headed out for the after-after party. I'll call you tomorrow to let you know who got drunk and who slept with whom."

They were laughing again as they disconnected the call. Her bestie had nothing to worry about. Sarai had no intentions of taking things to an extreme. But neither did she want to turn the exercise program back on. She got up from her office chair, on wobbly legs that still burned from the ten-minute contortions she'd endured, and made her way back to the forest inside the fridge.

CHAPTER FIVE

"*I* can't believe there's such a thing as a beauty blog." Reed leaned back in his desk chair as he looked at his computer screen. "And you make a living from it?"

"Yes, I do. I make a full time living hiding the flaws of women and ..." Sarai's smile warmed the low resolution of the screen. She leaned in conspiratorially. Reed found himself pitching forward too. "... and some men."

Reed threw his head back and laughed. He was used to being the one telling the jokes, and he did with Sarai. She laughed at all his jokes which was another point in her column. Reed was keeping score.

The dating app's algorithm said they were a 98%

compatibility match, but Reed wondered if it were actually an even 100%. Sarai was smart; she hadn't made a single spelling mistake or grammatical error in her profile. She was prompt; she always showed up a couple minutes early for their scheduled chats. And she was capable; she ran her own business and, by all accounts, was quite successful at it. Even if Reed didn't entirely understand it.

Yes. She was a perfect fit to be Mrs. Reed Cannon. Or Mrs. Austin-Cannon, if she preferred. Whatever she wanted to call herself, she was definitely taking his name.

"So, Sarai with an I ..."

"Yes, Reed with two E's?"

He looked up at the screen and smiled again. They'd only known each other for three weeks but they already had a running inside joke. Instead of the traditional spelling of Sarah with an H, her name ended in I. Reed was more often a last name instead of a first name, and traditionally it was spelled with an I instead of two E's.

In her profile, Sarai explained that her mother was of Middle Eastern descent; Saudi Arabian to be exact. And that's where the nontraditional spelling came from.

"You know," she said, "I almost didn't click on

your profile when I saw that you were a vet. I didn't think you'd want to date anyone with my heritage. Even though I was born here in America."

"I hold no ill will to the people of Afghanistan and Syria or any country in the Middle East. The peoples' countries have been taken over by radicals. Many of those citizens are just good people trying to live their lives."

When Reed had joined the army, helping people wasn't the first thing on his mind. He enjoyed the order that was inherent in the armed forces. The chain of command made sense to him. With the analytic mind he had, they'd put him in charge of tech. He'd been in Afghanistan helping to set up the communications system in a rebuilt community. He'd been working on setting up the new school for the children when the explosion happened that took his arm.

He crossed one arm over his chest. His fingers rubbed at his forearm, then caught the stump of his injury. "I was helping set up the internet when this happened."

Reed held up the stump to the computer's camera. He watched Sarai carefully as her gaze shifted on the computer screen. She blinked slowly and cocked her head slightly. Reed held still under her perusal. He felt the phantom sensation of his left-hand clenching into a fist.

"Does it hurt still?" Sarai asked.

Reed shook his head, wishing he could make his nonexistent fingers unball from a fist. But in his mind, his nails dug into his palm and the pain was real. "I didn't feel it when it was severed. And I didn't feel much after."

Sarai's gaze shifted back to center. She was looking directly at him again. She said nothing. She only waited.

He liked that about her. She didn't fill any silence unnecessarily. She didn't say anything cliché. It was another point in her favor. She was an excellent listener.

"Is that a dog barking?" she asked.

Reed bent down and scooped Soldier into the palm of his hand. The little Chihuahua weighed so little that it was easy to balance him in his palm. "Sarai meet Soldier. Salute, Soldier."

Soldier balanced on Reed's lap. He sat back on his hind legs and lifted his solitary front paw. Like Reed, Soldier had lost his left arm, allowing him the ability to still salute.

Sarai giggled with delight. "How did you two find each other?"

"He's not my dog. He belongs to the wife of one of the other soldiers here. We kinda took to each other."

"I can see why," Sarai said, leaving a long pause before filling in the silence. "You both have very serious faces."

Reed chuckled. He liked this girl more and more. Soldier stuck out his tongue and panted. Reed understood the sentiment.

"Listen, Sarai," Reed began again, trying to determine the right order of the words to ask her the question he'd been dying to ask since their first typed chat. Even then, with only characters standing in, she'd captured his full attention. "I'd love to see you."

Her gaze dipped down. Her smile loosened. "You're seeing me now."

She'd said she'd been burned before by the world of online dating. He had too. Women who were not who they said they were were a dime a dozen behind a computer screen. Then there were those that said they were okay with his shortcoming, as he liked to call it. Then they showed up and couldn't stop staring. Or they asked ridiculous and sometimes lewd questions, like what could he attach to his arm.

He'd taken his time with Sarai. But his time was running out. Reed had less than two months to court Sarai, woo her, and convince her to marry him.

He'd said on his profile that he was looking for a serious, long-term relationship. But he hadn't said how soon. Nor how serious.

"I want to take you out," he said.

"I told you, I'm out of town."

"But when you get back next week?" Reed watched her throat work. He wasn't imagining their chemistry. He knew they could be something more, something real if they could just meet in real life. Unless there was a reason they couldn't meet in person. "Sarai? Is there someone else?"

Her eyes flashed up to the screen. Indignation in the light green of them. "I wouldn't do that."

A small smile played at the edge of Reed's mouth. "I'm sorry. I just really like you, and I want to take this to the next level." Heck, he wanted to take it to the final level.

"We can see each other when I'm finished -I mean. We can see each other when I get back."

"So, next week?" Hope filled his heart.

She squirmed on the screen. "It might be a little longer. I'm working hard, trying to ... finish. But that doesn't mean I want to stop seeing you online, while I'm here, in this place."

Reed sighed. It would have to do. He could wait another week, a couple weeks if necessary. The moment she set foot back in Montana, he would sweep her off her feet. Metaphorically speaking since he only had one arm. Because he knew, without a doubt, that he wanted there to be nothing more than a hyphen between them.

CHAPTER SIX

*S*arai leaned back in her ergonomically correct chair. It squeaked, springs protesting the move. She ignored the sound in light of her new progress.

She hit post on her latest blog entry about finding your perfect shade of blush. Her last entry got over five thousand likes in just a week. She had a couple hundred comments on the post as well. Sarai had a knack for helping others enhance their outer beauty with the perfect shade or right accessory just by looking at their profile pictures.

She was feeling good today. She'd been doing well this whole last week. She'd made it further and further through the exercise video. Last night, she'd even made it to the end and was still standing ...

leaning against the sofa was more like it. But she was on her feet.

The greens in the fridge hadn't spoiled. She'd actually eaten them. They'd just needed a bit of spice, and olive oil, and a pinch of honey. With a bit of Middle Eastern flare, the field fare was edible. She'd even begun practicing mindful eating again like her doctor had taught her too.

Food was nourishment for the body, mind, and soul her psychologist used to tell her. But she'd be the first to admit that it tasted better with a bit of curry powder and cinnamon.

Her stomach grumbled now in the middle of her work day. Sarai saved her work and rose from her chair to answer its call. Mason had worried she would slip back into old, destructive patterns. He had nothing to worry about.

Coming from a world where she had to fit into the small sample-sized dresses made for mannequins, Sarai was often surprised she'd made it out of the modeling world with only a few scars. Unlike the other models during her tenure, Sarai hadn't developed bulimia or anorexia. Her affliction had been a bit different.

She passed Mason's bedroom door on the way to the kitchen. The door was ajar, likely the wind from last night. Mason liked to sleep with the windows and curtains thrown wide open. He never minded being on display.

Sarai reached in to pull the door closed when she caught sight of someone in the room.

There was a woman she didn't recognize standing in front of Mason's floor to ceiling mirrors. Her skin was tanned golden, as though she'd just come from the sands of Arabia. Her shoulders were elegant and proud, holding up a full bust. Her waist curved inward and then her hips flared out like the belly dancers her mother used to socialize with in Sarai's youth.

Sarai gasped, surprised to see that she was looking at herself. Had she changed so much since the last time she'd stood before a mirror? She'd learned in therapy that she didn't see herself as others did. She hadn't been in front of a full-length mirror in years.

It was only when she looked in a mirror that she had a problem. That's why there was only a hand mirror in her room and no full length mirror in her bathroom. Mason, on the other hand, had mirrors everywhere in his room, which was why Sarai avoided her roommate's private sanctuary like it was a bawdy house.

Intrigued by what she saw, Sarai took another step into Mason's room and then another. She walked on the balls of her toes, tip-toeing quietly into the room, as though afraid to spook her own reflection.

Sarai stood before the mirror and stared. It was like looking at a long lost friend. Granted, her top was flattering as it displayed her angular collar bones. And the leggings she wore held the rolls of flesh at bay. She wasn't flat everywhere as the photographers and designers desired.

Still, she looked … slimmer.

It was working. The change in her diet. The daily exercise. It was all working.

Making an impulsive decision, Sarai turned on her heel. She stepped away from Mason's wall to wall mirrors and opened another door. Inside Mason's bathroom was a scale. It sat catty-corner to the toilet as though it were simply a stepping stool for someone to do their business.

It had been at least three years since she'd stepped on a scale. The memory of the number it had last flashed at her still haunted her dreams some nights. But this was a new day. She'd seen her new reflection. Things were improving.

Sarai hesitated for a second. Then she took a

leap. She stepped onto the scale ... and wished she hadn't.

The number the needle landed on was higher than the last time she'd weighed herself years ago. Sarai's sucked in her gut, but it did no good. She felt nauseated as she peered down. The world spun as the needle rocked back and forth, landing at a higher number each time.

She reached out to the wall to steady herself. Then she decided to stop the torture and stepped off the scale. The needle fell like a stone back to zero, as though it had been straining under her massive weight, gasping for relief.

This was a disaster.

The mirror must've been a trick. Mason had probably gotten one of those slimming mirrors that department stores, and circuses, used to trick unsuspecting customers. That's the only explanation.

Sarai still felt the rolls on her abdomen. Her thighs still rubbed together creating enough friction to start an electric storm. The flesh at the back of her arms still flapped like wings that would never lift her bulk off the ground.

There were birds that couldn't fly because they

were fat. What were they? Ostriches? Yes, ostriches. Funny looking, long neck, fat-bellied ostriches.

There was no way Reed would want to kiss an ostrich. He couldn't get his arms around the bird's belly. He'd take one look at her flabby wings and run in the other direction.

Sarai's limbs felt heavier. Her gut felt bloated. She turned out of the bathroom, sure to avoid looking at the trick mirror. The ground shook at her retreat as the sliver of confidence she'd built over the last few days shattered.

Outside, a cloud settled over the once sunny day. Sarai's heart sped up even though her workout had been hours ago. Her limbs felt leaden. She just wanted to lie down, but her stomach continued its grumbling protest.

She couldn't face the bland greens today. She needed something to warm her insides and soothe her sad soul. She didn't get out much, preferring to interact with the world through her keyboard instead of face to face. But she was in need of some comfort, and food was the only friend she had to turn to.

CHAPTER SEVEN

*R*eed thumbed at the condensation on his mug. The frothy foam sat atop his drink. Tiny bubbles burst as they rose to the surface. He lifted his glass to meet the others around the table. The mugs crashed and the froth spilled over and onto the dining table.

"Here's to Dylan," said Xavier. "Our fearless leader."

"Hear, hear," came a chorus of male voices. Sean sat to one side of Reed. His shades were off, but he made sure that his scarred side was to the wall and not toward the diners in the restaurant. It had been like pulling teeth to get the man out of the house and off the ranch tonight.

The group was a sight when they went out in

force. Xavier and Fran got head nods from men and longing gazes from single women. Their wounds weren't possible to see out in public.

Sean, with his scars, got stares. Dylan, with his prosthetic leg, which he no longer bothered hiding under pants now that he had the love and admiration of a good woman, and Reed, with his prosthetic arm, got pointing and whispers.

Reed didn't let it get to him. Like all the men in his squad, he'd served his nation with honor. He'd left the people of his country a little safer and it had only cost him half a limb. Others had fared far worse. Some even paid the ultimate price.

"Much like the bomb that altered our lives," Xavier continued his boisterous toast. "Dylan had one moment of brightness, then he dimmed, and left behind a lot of smoke."

"You're terrible at this, you know?" said Fran.

"Oh, I'm getting to you," said X. This wasn't just Dylan's belated bachelor party. Francisco had gotten married shortly after Dylan took the proverbial leap. "And here's to Frances. Who followed behind Dylan into the belly of the institution of marriage."

"X," Reed cautioned his fellow soldier, but he knew it was a moot point. The guys loved to razz one another any chance they got.

"Don't get me wrong," said Xavier. "Marriage is a wonderful institution. I'm just not crazy enough to go inside."

No one laughed at Xavier's pathetic jokes. They all knew how he felt about marriage. The man was already eyeing the girls at the next table. And they were eyeing him back.

The five of them had all gathered for a rare night off the ranch for Dylan and Fran's belated bachelor parties. Both of their marriages had been so sudden that there had been no time to plan. Dr. Patel had insisted that they have a meal at his family restaurant on him. They were finally getting around to taking him up on it.

"Let me take this," said Reed, raising his glass once again. This time there was no crashing of mugs. The froth stayed inside everyone's container. "Dylan, we owe you our lives. You continue to lead us through dark times and show us the way. Not just on the battlefield, but in life. You came through adversity and were able to find the love of your life. I only hope I can do the same someday."

Dylan pressed his lips together and nodded. Gratitude was clear in his blue eyes. Reed turned his attention to Fran.

"Fran, your ability to plan, and your vision of a

better world, has touched more lives than you'll ever admit. You are a role model to the children now in your care, and to the children that will come onto the ranch for learning and healing. I am proud to be your brother, and hope that I can be half as good of a man to the family I plan to have someday."

Fran's throat worked. His Adam's apple bobbed up and down before he managed to swallow. Satisfied that he'd paid the proper tribute to his brothers, to his family, Reed raised his glass higher.

"To Dylan and Fran."

Xavier and Sean repeated Reed's words. But as soon as they were sipping at their brews, Xavier broke the moment, which wasn't a surprise.

"That's enough out of you Donna Reed," said Xavier. "As I was saying—"

"We're good, X, thanks," said Dylan. "Thank you, Reed. Those were powerful words."

Fran nodded his agreement. They both lifted their glasses to their lips again and drank. Each of their wedding bands caught in the low light of the restaurant.

Reed felt a pang in his heart and an itch on his finger. Though he no longer possessed his left hand, he still wanted to sport one of those bands.

"Looks like you're up next," Dylan said to Reed. "How's the online search for a wife going?"

"Things are going well," said Reed.

He'd been looking online for a while. There had been some time when he'd had plenty of horror stories to tell the guys about the desperate, unhinged, unsavory women trolling the interwebs. Story time hadn't happened for a while though.

Sarai had been in the first batch of online matches. Even though they'd been a near perfect match, she'd been hard to pin down. She still was. But like any problem, Reed knew there had to be a solution.

"You don't have a lot of time left," said Dylan. "It's less than six weeks before the zoning goes into effect on the ranch. It's going to take a year to fight it and get it changed after that deadline."

Reed nodded. He knew what was at stake. He was working on it. There were other women who were available as solutions. He just couldn't stop thinking about the one who was closest to him in every way but physically.

"Did we just hear you correctly?" said a feminine voice. The coeds who Xavier had been eyeing all night turned around to face their booth. "Did you say you have to get married to stay on your ranch?"

"Yes." Xavier pulled on a somber look that any cognizant woman would be able to see was fake. "We'll lose everything if we don't find brides."

These two girls, however, widened their gazes and cooed at the predicament. Reed knew that Xavier had been using this pickup line on unsuspecting women for weeks now. These two were just another group to take the bait.

"Wow," said one of them. She was curly haired and petite. "It's like something out of a romance novel."

"Did a grandfather write in his will that you can't inherit unless you get married by a certain age?" said the other. Her hair was long and bone-straight.

"Or are you all here in the country illegally?" said the one with the curls.

"No," said Reed. "We're all Army vets. It's a zoning issue."

The women's faces fell at the less than romantic legal issue the guys were facing.

"But," said the straight-haired one, "he just said you all need mail order brides."

"*We* don't." Fran held up his ringed finger.

Dylan followed suit, holding up his left hand.

Sean looked away.

With three out of five men off the table, the

women looked Reed's way to even up their numbers. Reed didn't have a piece of metal on his finger. He had a metal arm. He held up his prosthetic.

If the women glanced at it and didn't screech in horror, they might be worth his time.

"Oh, my God," said Curly Hair. Her screech was loud enough to force the cook to poke his head around the corner. "What happened to you?"

Her straight-haired friend reared back as though Reed might reach out and give her cooties with his metallic attachment.

Reed had just said that he was a veteran. Couldn't they put two and two together? Apparently not. "Alligator attack."

"Whoa," the two said in unison. Quieter, though.

Airheads weren't his cup of tea. Intelligent, humorous fan-girls were. Reed palmed the phone in his pocket. "Excuse me."

He got up from the table as Xavier crossed over to the girls' table.

Reed made his way to the back porch of the restaurant. A sappy country song about lovers constantly missing meeting each other played on the radio as he did. He dialed Sarai's number. He'd only dialed it one other time when their internet connection had been choppy.

It rang. Then rang some more. He was about to hang up when she answered.

"Reed?" She was a bit out of breath as she said his name.

"Hey," he said. His smile stretched wide just at the sound of her voice. Then he cursed under his breath. "It's midnight there, isn't it? I'm so sorry, I didn't consider the time difference."

"It's okay. I was up. I didn't know we were chatting tonight? I didn't have it on my schedule. I thought you were busy."

Just another thing he liked about this girl. She kept an orderly calendar.

"We're not. I am. I ... I was just thinking about you."

There was silence on the other end of the line. He heard traffic through the connection. Was she outside? Had he interrupted her evening? Was she with someone else?

She could be. She had every right to be. They'd never claimed exclusivity. He couldn't even call her his girlfriend.

"No, it's fine," she said. "I was just headed out to grab a bite."

"If you're on a date or something ..." Reed kicked at a pebble on the wood patio.

"I'm not seeing anyone else. I mean ..."

"Neither am I." Reed rushed to fill the silence, hoping he could close even more distance between him and this woman. "I don't want to see anyone but you."

There was more silence from her end, but he distinctly heard her breath catch. Had he gone too far? He didn't want to push her, even though his time was short. This thing between him and Sarai was too important to mess up over a zoning deadline.

"I'm sorry," said Reed. "I'm not trying to rush you. I just ... am I the only one who feels something here?"

"No."

Her voice was so quiet; he wasn't sure he'd heard her until she repeated herself.

"No, you're not."

There was more silence on the line. But it was a comfortable silence. It was the silence they'd shared a couple of times online when she'd caught him gazing at her. There was a hint of embarrassment in her tone, but also pleasure.

"Listen," said Reed. "I don't want to hold you up from your meal. I just wanted to hear your voice."

He could practically hear her smiling through the phone. He knew exactly what that would look like. Her beautiful face would stretch over perfectly straight, white teeth. Her eyes would crinkle at the corners. She might run her hands over her ear to brush away a nonexistent stray hair.

"I'll call you tomorrow."

"Okay," she said. "Goodnight, Reed."

"Good morning, Sarai."

"What?"

"It's already a new day there, in Paris, right?"

"Oh. Right. Of course."

Reed chuckled. He loved getting her all flustered. She'd look away from the screen when she did, giving him a moment to stare at her without shame. Soon he would be able to tilt up her chin when she looked down.

Reed hit the END button on his phone. But he knew that wasn't the end. It didn't matter when it started, but he knew he wanted to begin with this girl and never end. Even if that meant he'd have to leave the ranch.

CHAPTER EIGHT

*S*arai hit the END button on her phone. The cool night air slapped her in the face. She hated lying to Reed. Heck, she hated lying to herself.

She'd promised herself that she'd get the weight off in the next few weeks so that she could be confident when she presented herself to him. So that she could be the girl she used to be before it all came crashing down one day on a photo shoot.

But here she was; Week One of her promise, and she hadn't even made any progress. In fact, she was a few steps back. What was she going to do?

Her stomach grumbled again, letting her know what it wanted to do. The smell of curry and spice didn't warm her as she'd hoped it would. The thought of putting the rich cream and carb-loaded rice in her body made her want to puke.

She couldn't go in there. She couldn't eat that food. The day of the photo shoot, she'd met the designer's weight goal after only consuming liquids. Maybe if she just did a little abstinence from food, for just a few days, she could get on track.

Her phone rang at that instant. Mason's made-up face popped on the Caller ID, like a virtual angel on her shoulder hearing her naughty thoughts. Sarai hit DECLINE.

She wasn't regressing into old, harmful ways. She had tools. She knew how to manage her food intake. But it would be okay if she took a day off or two. Fasting was entirely safe if done correctly.

The sounds of a country song of two lovers constantly missing meeting one another sounded into the quiet of the night. It was a peculiar thing to hear the crooning of a cowboy coming out of the doors of an Indian Restaurant.

"Sarai, is that you?"

Was everyone checking up on her tonight? First, Reed. Then Mason, and now her former psychologist.

Sarai turned a model bright smile on, complete with smizing of the eyes—as Tyra Banks liked to say

—as she turned to greet Dr. Patel. "Dr. Patel, hi, I thought you spent Wednesday nights at church."

She'd counted on that. She'd learned her mindful eating at Patel's Family Restaurant. Back when Dr. Patel had diagnosed her, one of the treatments was to come dine with him and his family there on Thursday nights.

At Patel's, Sarai had learned to take comfort in curries and chutneys. She'd learned that bread wasn't the devil and a warm piece of garlic naan was sweeter and more satisfying than a bar of chocolate. She'd learned to take thirty minutes just to eat a bowl of rice, reveling in each grain as it hit her tongue.

Mindful Eating, Dr. Patel had called it. It was how Sarai had reclaimed her life after the incessant rejection of modeling had changed her perception of herself. It was how she'd learned to use food to heal and not harm her body.

"It's been too long." Dr. Patel opened his arms up to her. The man was a hugger. But he was also a good listener with a great memory.

He didn't bring her into a hug. He rested his hands lightly on her shoulders and gave her a squeeze. After years of being nothing more than a mannequin for clothes, makeup, and accessories,

Sarai still didn't take to people touching her without her permission. She'd given Dr. Patel this permission long ago. Still, he was not one to cross boundaries. He'd wait until his permission was renewed.

"Are you coming in to eat?" he asked.

"I ..." Sarai opened her mouth and caught the whiff of the spices that had warmed her from the inside out when she was healing. But she also caught sight of her reflection in a car window. "I was just passing by. I thought you were in church on Wednesdays."

"It's a special day. Some good friends of mine are having a celebration. Why don't you come inside? I'd love for you to meet them."

Sarai was already backing away. "No, I was just out for a walk."

Dr. Patel nodded. But though his head acquiesced, his eyes saw deeper. "How are you adjusting to everyday life?"

"I'm doing okay." Sarai shrugged. The movement might've been hard to see in the voluminous hoodie she was wearing along with the two-sizes too big sweatpants. Dr. Patel wasn't looking at her body. He looked in her eyes.

"How is your heart?" he asked. "Are you getting out? Meeting new people?"

"I'm dating." Not exactly getting out, but online dating was the new age version of going to bars and clubs to meet people.

"How does this gentleman make you feel?"

Sarai smiled thinking about Reed. "He gets me. He listens to me. He's so easy to talk to."

"There it is." Dr. Patel put his index finger under her chin and lifted. "You glow just talking about him. The way you feel inside lights you up outside."

Sarai did feel warm inside when she talked about Reed. She just wished that warmth inside her would burn some extra calories.

"I can't say I'm not disappointed," said Dr. Patel. "I wanted to set you up with a young man who I thought would be perfect for you."

Sarai cringed. Soon after she'd completed her treatment for her eating disorder with Dr. Patel, he'd begun talking about how she now needed to heal her heart. He'd wanted her to come to his church to meet people then. Sarai had demurred then, still getting used to the new her.

"It looks like I'm too late though," said Dr. Patel. But he didn't sound the least bit put out. He smiled when he admitted his defeat. "I can't wait to meet this young man who's stolen your heart."

CHAPTER NINE

*a*fter a year of ranch-style living, a three-story walk-up seemed like a hassle to Reed. Standing in the one-bedroom apartment, he crossed the linoleum floor to the barred window.

Outside, the view was nothing but concrete. There were no rolling pastures like on the ranch. No sounds of animals roaming about or calling to each other. Instead, the honks of horns and walla walla of the inner city yelled at him.

Instead of looking out to see Xavier and Sean shooting hoops, Reed saw skinny, young boys with pants hanging low on their hips and angry tattoos on their bare, bird-like chests.

He didn't catch Dylan and Maggie sneaking a kiss behind the barn, or Fran and Eva holding hands as they walked down the lane. Nope. Instead, he saw young girls in too much makeup and too tight jeans talking to grown men twice their age.

Instead of a pack of tame disabled dogs rambling about at the feet of a group of humans who cared for them, Reed looked down to witness young boys holding dogs on short leashes as the canines gnashed their teeth and snarled at one another. Life off the ranch was truly a different world.

"Now we do have wheelchair access. But it's around the back."

Reed turned from the window to face the landlord of the complex. The man was short with a beer belly and ketchup stains on the collar of his shirt.

"There's nothing wrong with my legs," said Reed.

The landlord glanced at Reed's pants-covered legs. A second too late, the man jerked his gaze back up, skirting over Reed's prosthetic. "Well, of course not. I wasn't implying that there was. I just want you to know that we are up to code with the Fair Housing Act and all that mumbo jumbo."

The Fair Housing Act was not mumbo jumbo. It was the law. A law that the federal government deemed necessary to put in place to protect the rights of people of different races, color, religion, national origin, gender, familial status, and ability.

Reed had been around the back of the complex to use that particular entrance, not because he needed it. He'd seen an elderly woman with two bags of groceries. He'd offered his help, but when she'd caught sight of Reed's arm, she'd hesitated. Reed, in his typical fashion when someone was uncomfortable with his wound, made a joke.

"Don't worry, I can handle the bags. I'm all right." He waved his fully intact right arm.

The old lady didn't get it. But she did offer him her bags.

As they made their way up the concrete ramp of the handicap entrance, Reed noted all the cracks in the walkway. Someone in a wheelchair would have great difficulty navigating this place. Someone who needed a cane to get around, someone who had to watch their step to avoid a fall, would face the same challenges.

The law wasn't just for those missing limbs or who had challenges with mobility. Clearly, the landlord had done the bare minimum and called it a day. Whether he put down a deposit on the apartment or not, Reed would definitely be filing a complaint in the morning.

"You'll be happy to know there's a bus on the corner, son. In case you were worried about getting around."

Just as much as Reed hated being underestimated, he hated being called son by anyone he wasn't related to. He'd endured it with a few drill sergeants and other superiors in the service. He'd never balk against the chain of command. But it still got under his skin.

"I can drive," he said to the landlord as he made his way towards the bedroom.

"Really? Is that safe?"

Reed didn't answer. He looked into the bedroom.

"Now, son, any other modifications you have to make, like something to hold you up while you take a shower, you'll be responsible for putting in and taking down when you leave."

"I don't need to make any other accommodations. It's just my arm."

Reed held up his fully functioning right arm. That confused the landlord, who again looked at his prosthetic. Then immediately jerked his gaze away.

Reed didn't expect the man to get the joke. He didn't expect that anyone in this neighborhood would understand him. They'd likely ask a lot of questions or stare and point. He'd stick out like a sore thumb because he only had one.

Still, Reed sighed and took the application the landlord offered. He didn't have many options. Even if he moved off the ranch, he'd still have to commute there every weekday. That's where his job was. Finding a job for a one-armed computer tech was going to be a stretch, and he knew it. The money he got from the government, coupled with what he earned from his work on the ranch, wouldn't afford him any luxuries.

Reed ignored the few stares he got as he made his way back to his truck. It didn't stop his new neighbors from looking at him as though he were less than a man. All because he was missing one of his four limbs. They couldn't see that there wasn't much that limited him. The only thing holding him back in his life was not proposing to the woman he fully expected to spend the rest of his life with.

Reed and Sarai had been talking every morning for the past week. They spoke early in the mornings due to the time difference. Every day he'd wanted to bring up the zoning issue on the ranch and casually work in his need to get married. But he didn't want his proposal to hinge on the zoning issue. He was convinced he wouldn't find a better woman for him than Sarai, not in the cyber world or the real world. So, he'd wait until she came back.

He had to postpone their talk this morning to take this appointment. She hadn't protested, saying she had work to do and could use the time. But they were back on schedule tomorrow. He would broach the topic with her then. Not about the zoning. But definitely about their relationship status.

Could he claim her as his girlfriend even though they hadn't met in person? Maybe he could even fly over to France this weekend. It would cost him the deposit on the apartment, but it would be worth it to see her in the flesh.

Reed's phone rang and his heart pounded at the sound. Could it be her? Was she calling him in spite of their later date? He fished the device out of his pocket hoping to see Sarai's smiling face in the caller ID. Instead, he saw Fran's mug.

"Yeah?" Reed leaned against the passenger side of his truck as he pressed the phone to his ear.

"Hey, you still in town?"

"Just about to head back."

"Eva's got a flat. I'm all the way on the other side of town. Do you think you could give her a hand changing the tire?"

The knot that had lodged itself between Reed's

shoulder blades during his apartment visit and tour of his new neighborhood loosened. He felt the phantom pain in his long-lost hand relax. "You know I've only got one of those."

Fran made an impatient sound. "I'm serious, man."

Reed knew Fran was serious. His brothers didn't think twice about his ability to do what was necessary. Something as simple as changing a tire, a feat which most four-limbed human beings couldn't do with two hands, they thought nothing of asking a one-armed man to perform.

"I'm on my way to her," Reed said. He disconnected and hopped in behind the wheel.

He found Eva fifteen minutes later. She was parked near Patel's. Reed greeted the petite brunette with a grin and a hug.

"I told Fran that I could've called Triple-A," she said.

Reed made the same impatient sound that Fran had made a quarter hour ago over the phone. Eva was fiercely independent. She was slowly learning that all the men on the ranch would move heaven and earth for each other and the ones they loved. Reed wanted Sarai to experience the same devotion.

Sarai had told him that her parents traveled a lot

and they didn't spend time together. Reed had assumed her parents were divorced but was surprised to learn that they weren't. They simply crossed paths whenever their work put them in the same country.

He couldn't understand how that worked. Once he and Sarai were on the same continent he was determined to have her close by his side. The idea of flying to France was looking more and more appealing to him each moment.

For now, Reed set to work changing Eva's tire. But when he pulled out the spare, he saw that it, too, was flat.

"We can wait for Fran to bring another spare. Or we can leave it here and come back for it tomorrow."

"I just got this car," moaned Eva.

"Yeah, but you insisted on getting a used car with your own money instead of letting your husband buy you a brand new one."

"I don't need a new car."

Eva was a notorious penny pincher. Fran had a habit of telling his wife something was used or discounted when it wasn't just to weaken the fight he'd get out of her. Reed suspected this new used car would stay here on the side of the road, leaving Fran the perfect excuse to buy his frugal wife a brand new model.

"I'm so sorry to take you out of your way," said Eva.

"You know it was no trouble. And I'd never leave you stranded."

"You've got crud all over your shirt because of me." Eva wiped at the grease stain on his shirt.

Reed caught Eva's fingers in his hand and tugged her to move forward. "Why don't you pay me back with dinner. Patel's is just around the corner."

"Deal. Thanks for coming out. You're my hero." Eva pecked the side of Reed's cheek.

Reed leaned into her affectionate embrace. Eva was maternal to her core. Reed would miss her and Maggie fussing over him daily. But he wanted his own wife to fuss over him.

He placed Eva in the crook of his good arm and they fell into step with one another. As they turned the corner, another woman bumped into his chest. The bag of food she'd been carrying fell out of her hands and splattered onto the ground. The smell of curry and other spices wafted through the air.

"I'm so sorry …" Reed began and then trailed off. It couldn't be. He was hallucinating. "Sarai?"

CHAPTER TEN

*S*arai's entire life flashed before her eyes.
She saw herself at seven when her
mother first pushed her onto the stage at beauty
pageants when she just wanted to hang out with her
friends playing Barbies. She felt the ache in her jaw
at seventeen from smiling at casting call after casting
call where she was poked, prodded, pinched, and
spoken about as though she wasn't there. She
smelled the rancid smell of coffee and cola and
cigarettes at twenty-one as she crammed her body
into dresses a size too small and heels too narrow.

As the scenes of her short life flashed before her
eyes, Sarai felt the agony of drowning in tears of the
rejection, of the loneliness, of the constant hunger of
modeling. That pain of not being good enough had

been clawing its way back into her consciousness over the past week as she tried and failed to exercise. As she tried and failed to eat mindfully. As she tried and failed to lose the weight she'd learned to accept was normal and healthy.

She'd taken to looking in the mirror at the evidence again. She'd taken to stepping on the scale and seeing the cold hard facts. She'd thought she'd gained a new lease on life during her therapy. The truth was that all she'd gained was weight.

Her reflection in the glass, the numbers on the scale, they told a different story. They told the story of a once beautiful girl who had let herself go. All she'd gained over the last couple of years was weight. The weight that wasn't coming off. The weight that would keep her from receiving the real live affection of any man, including the one who was now standing in front of her.

"Sarai, is that you?"

Was it her? Was this woman standing before him the real Sarai Austin? She didn't feel like herself. She'd been fasting for the last five days. When she'd stepped on the scale this morning it had gone up two pounds instead of falling even a single ounce. Devastation didn't begin to describe how she felt.

She had to face facts. She wasn't going to lose

this weight. She'd let it hang around too long. And now it weighed her down heavily on the sidewalk outside of Patel's standing in a puddle of curried rice and buttered chicken that she wouldn't even get to eat.

And Reed was standing there, looking down on her. Standing with a petite, skinny woman with a bright smile and big eyes. Her waist was small and her hips flared. She wasn't model tall, but she had the kind of figure men were now clamoring over on social media. And she was in Reed's arms.

Sarai couldn't muster the energy to run. All she could do was stand there with the late day sun glaring brightly in her face.

When a cloud moved in she saw clearly. When he said her name, she knew for sure. The life she'd been trying to carve for herself by shaving off the pounds, that life was over.

"I can't believe it," Reed continued.

Sarai waited for the shouting to start. Surely his anger would burst forward now that she'd been caught in a web of lies. Or worse, what if he simply recoiled from her, walked around her, and never spoke to her again. It would be a far worse rejection than any agent or fashion designer or photographer. Because she did want to stand in Reed's light.

"Is this why you couldn't talk today?" he asked, "Because you were flying back?"

Sarai hadn't been able to talk with Reed today because she was under a work deadline that she'd put off all week. It was highly unlike her to miss a deadline, but her body image and weight issues had consumed her. The only time she had felt a semblance of normality was in her morning talks with Reed. And the more she talked to him, the more guilty she felt.

It was a vicious cycle. She'd been spinning around so fast that she just needed for it all to stop.

She'd spent the entire day yesterday in bed. Then, this morning, she'd woken up and forced out a blasé post about choosing the best toner to contour a thin nose.

The art of contouring was just a diversion away from the truth. At the end of the night, the makeup came off, and the big nose would be revealed every time. She wasn't fooling anyone. She was still waiting for her readers to call her out on it. But as yet, no one had.

"This is the best surprise," said Reed. He was smiling at her, not sneering, not glaring, not even frowning. His handsome face was even handsomer in person. And then she was in his arms.

Reed let go of the petite brunette and pulled Sarai into a one-armed hug. But even with that single arm Sarai felt enveloped. She felt surrounded by him.

Her arms came around his back as her sneakered feet squished in her ruined dinner. Reed's shoulders were broad. He smelled like a fresh breeze and warm bread. Sarai wanted to take a bite.

He wasn't angry with her. He thought she'd just returned from her fake trip. He still didn't realize she'd been here all the time, hiding because she was ashamed of the way she looked.

Then she realized. She still looked the way she looked. Even worse, she was in an unflattering sweat suit with minimal makeup.

Of course, she'd put on blush, mascara, and a bit of gloss. She wasn't a savage. But she'd done no contouring, and she had on no eyeshadow.

She was a mess. And the guy of her dreams was gazing down at her. But he wasn't looking at her sweatshirt where her uniboob made an impression in the cotton. He wasn't looking down at the baggy sweatpants that made her look two sizes bigger.

No, he was looking at her face. He was looking into her eyes. And he was smiling with a smile huge enough for her to fall in.

"I'm so happy to see you, Sarai."

And at that moment, Sarai no longer wanted to hide. She didn't care that the flesh of her arms flapped against his back. She didn't care that her stomach pushed against the elastic of her waistband. She didn't care that if she moved her thunder thighs would crack the pavement.

All she cared about was standing under Reed's smiling gaze. And she'd do anything to stay in this exact spot for the rest of her life.

CHAPTER ELEVEN

*I*t was like one of those moments when he was dreaming and he knew he was dreaming and he could direct the course of his dreams. Reed had been dreaming about Sarai for weeks. Nothing X-rated. Just dreams of being in her presence, holding her, talking to her, sitting beside her, holding her hand. Most of the dreams didn't even end with a kiss.

This—the embrace he held her in right now— this was a dream come true. He didn't want to wake up. He didn't want to let her go.

If he'd had any doubts about her, which he didn't, he was certain now. The reality of Sarai, the smell of her, the feel of her, the small gasp she let out as he gave her warm body a squeeze, let him know that this was the real deal.

"I'm so happy to see you, Sarai," he said when he finally was able to let her go. "I can't believe you're standing here in front of me."

"Yeah. Yeah well, as you said, I couldn't talk to you this morning because I was coming here. Home. I've come back home. Unexpectedly. And it looks like I've surprised you."

She had surprised him. But why had her voice taken on a sour note? Reed noticed that Sarai's gaze had slid past him and was now darting at something behind him. At someone behind him.

Eva stood watching the whole exchange with interest. Reed knew this whole incident would be spread around the ranch in just a matter of seconds once she whipped out her phone and texted Fran. That was the payoff for living in close quarters.

He didn't blame Eva. He'd do the same if he had a juicy tidbit about one of the others. It was something Sarai would have to get used to when she came into their group.

A thought entered Reed's mind. A thought he hadn't dared to consider until now. There was time.

There was enough time to convince Sarai that they were right for each other. Not for right now but for always. He had just over a month to take her on a few dates, sweep her off her feet, and then pop the question. Not because he had to, but because he wanted to.

Reed didn't knock arranged marriages and marriages of convenience. But this—what he felt for Sarai—this was something else. He couldn't call it love at first sight. Even though this was the first time he was seeing her live and in the flesh. He'd fallen for her just through their conversations, and he believed she'd done the same.

So why was she fidgeting and not meeting his gaze? Because her gaze was still darting behind him. At Eva.

She couldn't think that— That he could possibly — Didn't she know that he wasn't the kind of guy to lie or cheat?

Reed reached back with his prosthetic and motioned to Eva. "Sarai Austin, I'd like you to meet Eva DeMonti, Fran's wife."

"Fran's wife?" said Sarai.

Reed heard the relief rush through her voice. She had doubted him. He couldn't understand why. He'd have to work harder to make sure she knew how much she meant to him.

Eva stepped forward with a welcoming, nonthreatening smile of a woman who was not after a man. The two women shook hands. Then Eva's eyes went large.

"Wait?" said Eva. "Sarai Austin? The model?"

It was almost imperceptible. Reed probably wouldn't have noticed it except he was staring so intently at Sarai. He saw her shoulders hunch at Eva's recognition.

Reed had known Sarai was a model. She'd mentioned it in her profile. But he couldn't remember them talking about it in any of their conversations. She'd only ever mentioned her beauty blog.

"That was a lifetime ago." Sarai wrapped her arms around her figure as though she were trying to hide herself.

"I know," said Eva. "Now you do a makeup blog. You taught me how to do the smoky eye."

Eva waved her fingers in front of her eyes and widened her gaze. Reed hadn't noticed that there was coloring on the lids of Eva's eyes until just now.

"It looks really good," said Sarai, a small smile on her face as she narrowed her gaze at Eva's eyes. "You have a really nice tilt to your eyes. You should elongate the corners with a thin pencil to accentuate that."

"Good tip," said Eva.

Reed had no idea what the two women were on about. He only knew he wanted to spend more time with Sarai, preferably alone so he could start his campaign to win her hand.

"Maybe you could show me how sometime?" Eva continued. "If you ever come to the ranch."

Sarai looked uncertainly at Reed.

"Yes, you should come out to the ranch," said Reed. "I was just about to take Eva back. You could come with us."

"Oh, I'm not dressed to go out," said Sarai.

She looked beautiful to him. Even in the jogging pants and the oversized sweatshirt. Besides, the ranch wasn't a place for fancy dressing. But he didn't want their first time in each other's presence to be spoiled by meeting his entire squad and their even more meddlesome wives.

"Why don't you come to grab a bite at Patel's with us," said Reed. "It's the least I can do since I'm responsible for ruining your dinner."

"It's okay," she said, looking down at the curry-stained paperbag on the sidewalk. "It wasn't for me. I mean, I shouldn't have gotten it anyway."

Reed frowned at that statement. Instead of pursuing dinner at the restaurant, which she did not seem open to, he decided on another route. "Can I give you a lift home?"

Sarai blinked at him, as though she didn't understand the question. Her gaze slid down his arm, his prosthetic arm.

"I do have my driver's license." He felt his jaw tighten and tried to loosen it.

But Sarai didn't look at him in shock. Realization dawned in her green eyes. A small sigh escaped her lips. He knew that sigh. It was the sound she made before she launched a counter-attack on whatever debate they were having.

"Oh, no," she said. "It's just that I'm not that far. I live in walking distance."

"Well, can I walk with you?"

Sarai took a deep breath this time. This sound was new to Reed. It sounded to him as though she were summoning courage. He couldn't imagine what there was to be brave about.

She squared her shoulders, stepped back, and opened her arms. "Are you sure?"

Reed didn't hesitate. "Of course I'm sure."

Sarai's hands dropped to her sides. Reed couldn't see her curves due to the excessive cloth covering her skin, but he knew they were there. He was more intent on looking into her eyes. He could get lost in her gaze.

With her arms at her sides, she still looked at him as though she were confused. But then she nodded in acceptance. "Okay then."

Reed turned to Eva and handed her his car keys. "Order mine to go. I'll be back in a bit."

"Take your time." Eva grinned.

Reed turned back to Sarai. He offered her his arm. His heart stopped when she hesitated again.

But she wasn't looking at his prosthetic. She was looking into his eyes, searching for something. He supposed she found whatever she was looking for because she slipped her hand in the crook of his elbow where he still had flesh. Reed's entire body came alive with just that small touch.

CHAPTER TWELVE

*S*arai kept her arms wrapped tight around her middle. She hoped against hope that the maneuver had a slimming effect on her rotund body. But she doubted it.

With every lift of her foot, she felt the jiggle of her upper thighs rubbing together. With every foot placed in front of the other, she heard the ground shake. Could Reed hear it too?

He must have with the way he was fidgeting. He tugged at his ear with his right hand. Then he adjusted a mechanism on his prosthetic.

Sarai marveled at how realistic the fingers looked. The only thing that gave them away was the fact that they weren't twitching like the fingers of his right hand. Reed reached the apparatus out to her and Sarai jerked, embarrassed that she'd been staring.

"I'm sorry." Reed pulled his hand away. "It's just that you're walking on the outside of the sidewalk and closer to the cars. My father beat into my head that a gentleman always puts himself in front of danger for a lady."

Sarai hadn't been considering her safety when she'd chosen which side of the sidewalk to walk on. She'd only been considering her angles. Her right side was her best side. She'd learned through her years of modeling. She needed every advantage she could get.

But she allowed Reed to cross over to the left side of her. He placed both his arms behind his back as they walked. Sarai busied herself trying to angle her body as she walked so that he got a view of her right side, her better side. Her machinations had her walking straight into a pole.

Reed put his prosthetic arm out in front of her, between her and the tree stump of a pole. Her belly impacted the prosthetic and bark scraped against the fake arm.

"I'm so, so sorry." Sarai stepped back, rearranging her sweatshirt to hide the evidence of the rolls. But she knew he'd already felt them. Or if not felt them, he had to have felt the impact. There were wood chippings along the arm.

"Did I hurt you?" he asked.

Shouldn't she be asking him that question? But he simply flicked the pieces of bark from his prosthetic and focused his gaze on her. Again, on her face, not her body.

She wasn't even wearing full makeup, but he didn't seem to notice. She'd never believed that about guys, that they didn't notice makeup. But it must be true with Reed. His smile was bright and genuine and ... interested.

"How was your flight?"

Sarai gulped before she let loose the lie. Her tongue was feeling heavier than her frame. "It was fine."

"Nasty airplane food? Is that why you were at Patel's?"

"I shouldn't have gone there. I'm on a diet."

Reed frowned down at her, finally looking somewhere that wasn't her eyes.

Sarai held her breath. She sucked it in. But who was she kidding?

Reed shook his head. "I've never understood the concept of diets. It must be a girl thing."

Sarai stared at him. Maybe he was blind? Did he not see the colossal weight she was carrying around?

"I'm sorry, was that sexist?" he said with a deprecating smile. "I just don't believe in depriving myself. That's why I wanted to see you sooner rather than later. You know I was actually contemplating flying out to Paris this weekend?"

Sarai's heart quickened, faster than it had when she'd been moving along to that exercise video. Could falling for a guy be considered as a workout? Because if so, she would lose the weight in no time under Reed's attention.

"Anyway, Patel's is one of my favorite restaurants," he said. "I'm there all the time."

"I used to go there all the time during therapy."

"Therapy?"

Her racing heartbeat slowed as her chest tightened. She didn't want to tell another lie. They were starting to weigh her down more than her weight. "I told you that I was a model. I had to deal with a lot of rejection. So my parents sent me to a psychologist."

"Rejection? I don't see how when you're so beautiful."

"Are you blind? I'm not even wearing blush."

Reed peered down at her cheeks. "Would that

make a difference? Maybe I am blind. They say the physical vanishes when you see a person for who they are inside."

And now she was out of breath. Yes, falling for Reed Cannon was definitely a workout. If not the pounds, she would surely lose her heart to this guy. "It was called food therapy. Mindful eating."

"That sounds like something Dr. Patel would make his patients do."

"You know Dr. Patel?"

Reed nodded. "He works on the ranch. And he's my psychologist."

"Mine, too. Or at least he was. I finished therapy a year ago."

"How do we have all these connections in real life and yet we meet online?"

"It's crazy, isn't it?"

"Obviously must be if we've both needed a psychologist," he grinned. "Dr. Patel helped a lot with my PTSD and coping with the loss of my limb."

He held up his prosthetic arm. He was watching her face again, carefully. Sarai wasn't sure what he was looking for. She only hoped that he found it.

"This is me," she said as they came up to her place.

"It suits you," Reed said looking at the townhouse she shared with Mason.

Sarai wasn't watching where she was going again, and she stumbled as she came to the stairs of the stoop. Reed reached out for her with both arms. She felt the hard, cold material of his prosthetic at the fleshy parts of her side.

Oh, no. Her sweatshirt had ridden up. Reed was touching her fat. Sarai jerked away.

Reed pulled his prosthetic arm away from her and then placed it behind his back. "I'm sorry."

"No, I'm sorry. This isn't what I planned. It's not how I planned to meet you. I thought there would be more time for me to prepare for this."

He looked down at his arm. "I understand."

But Sarai didn't think he did. He deserved to know the truth. She didn't want there to be any more excess layers between them than there already were. She needed to come clean.

"Listen, Sarai, there's something I haven't told you."

And she would come clean. Right after he did. It was polite to take turns.

"There's a reason I went to the dating site in the first place. It was to find a wife."

He paused and in his pause Sarai blinked her eyes rapidly searching for clarity. She would've tugged at her ears to be sure she'd heard him correctly.

Did he just say that he was looking for a wife?

"I need to get married to stay on the ranch," Reed continued.

"You're getting married?"

"I'll need to if I want to stay there."

She knew it was too good to be true. The guy of her dreams was getting married. Her heart should've slowed to a complete halt. Instead, it continued to race as though it could run after him and hold onto him for herself.

"Anyway, I've got six weeks," he said. "I need to find a bride in a little less than six weeks or move."

Need to? As in present tense? So he hadn't found someone? She wasn't too late? "Six weeks?"

"I know it's fast. I know it's sudden. But I think there's something here, between us."

"Us?"

"Yes, us. My plan was to date you, to woo you, and then to pop the question."

Sarai couldn't swallow past the lump in her throat. She tried to force out something more than a single syllable but failed.

"I realize that six weeks is too sudden," Reed continued. "So, I've decided that I can wait."

The words burst out of her now. "Wait? Why? Why wait?"

"I just ... Well, you don't think it's too soon for us? We literally just met."

"You were thinking of asking me to marry you?"

"Well ... I ... it's just that we're so compatible. Statistically speaking, I won't find a better match than you. So, it just makes sense on an analytical level."

Now her heart did stop. Her breathing stopped. She stopped blinking. Sarai held entirely and completely still in this moment, committing every detail to memory.

The way Reed chewed at the corner of his lip. The way he ran his right hand through his hair. The way his left arm was behind his back, as though he were prepared to bow like a gentleman of old days. And the way he looked at her like she was something special.

No one had looked at her like she was something special in so long.

"And," he continued, "there's the fact that I really, really like you."

Sarai nodded. She took a deep breath in as she

contemplated his words. When she had her answer, she spoke slowly and surely. "If you ask me in six weeks, the answer will be the same. So, logically, you might as well ask me now and be able to stay on the ranch."

Reed stared at her. He took a step back, looking her up and down. Sarai began to squirm and fidget under his perusal. Was he finally coming to his senses?

No. He was going down on bended knee.

"Sarai Austin, you captured my attention with your profile blurb. Then you held it with our chats and conversations. Will you do me the honor of becoming my partner IRL?"

This was happening. It was really happening. Sarai pushed past the lump in her throat and managed a choked yes.

Reed's smile was so big, so huge. Sarai wanted to make him smile like that for the rest of her days. And she would. She would be the woman he deserved to have. Inside and out.

Six weeks had been unrealistic for such a life-changing event. They had time now. She had time now. Time to be the woman she knew she could be.

CHAPTER THIRTEEN

One thing that was hard for a one-armed man to do was to tie a knot. On this big day, for Reed, a clip-on simply would not do. Xavier wound the fabric around Reed's neck and made a noose.

"You sure about this?" asked Xavier as he tightened the tie.

"I've never been more certain." Reed held still as his friend perfected the knot. He tilted up his chin so he could glance in the mirror at his reflection.

"You just met this girl. Are you sure you know everything you need to know about her?"

"I've known Sarai for almost a month. That's longer than Dylan knew Maggie, or Fran knew Eva and looked how that worked out for all of them. Then there's the math."

"Right, the math." Xavier gave a tug of the knot. "The basis of every good relationship."

"Math doesn't lie."

"Math is quantitative," said Xavier, "not qualitative. What do you really know about this girl?"

"We have a lot in common."

"The fact that she knows obscure facts in the Whoverse does not necessarily make you compatible."

"She gets me," said Reed. "I get her. Neither of us is perfect. But what faults may come about either of us, I'm still ninety-eight percent sure she's the one for me."

"Not one-hundred?"

"It's statistically impossible to get a perfect score."

From the corner of the room, Soldier barked as though he agreed. Reed bent down to the dog and offered his hand. The dog hopped up on his hind legs and tapped Reed's open palm with his sole front paw in their version of a high five.

"I am not going to be upstaged by a dog." Xavier

held out his palm and Reed clasped it in his own. "All right. I'll have your back."

With his free hand, Xavier gave Reed a firm pat on his back. Reed didn't return the favor. That's where Xavier's scars were. They weren't painful any longer. But like all of the soldiers that came to this ranch, Xavier was cognizant of his own wounds.

"I know you've got my back, bro," said Reed. "I just wish you'd consider staying here."

Xavier shook his head. "You know marriage isn't for me. But don't worry. You'll still get shared custody of me. You guys will have me on the weekends."

There was a knock at the door. Reed thought for a second that it might be one of the other soldiers, but he dismissed that idea. None of them would bother to knock. They'd just barge in.

Dr. Patel poked his gray head in the door with his fatherly smile. "Good morning, Specialist Ramos. Might I have a private word with the man of the hour?"

With one final adjustment of Reed's tie, Xavier headed out the door. Dr. Patel came in, closing the door behind him. He didn't take a seat but stood smiling proudly at Reed.

Dr. Patel had made such a positive impact in

everyone on the ranch's lives. He'd worked tirelessly and patiently to ensure the men were healed from the inside out. He'd officiated Dylan's and Fran's weddings. And now, he would join Reed and Sarai together in holy matrimony.

"Is it time?" Reed heard the eagerness in his own voice.

"Almost," said Dr. Patel. "I just wanted to have a little chat with you."

Neither Reed's or Sarai's parents could make it to the ceremony on such short notice. Neither parents were particularly happy about the quickness of the marriage. Well, his parents weren't. Sarai had mentioned that she'd emailed her parents but hadn't heard back yet.

Reed had proposed just two days ago and it had been a whirlwind of preparations since. He'd hardly seen Sarai during that time as Maggie and Eva had insisted on shopping trips with his bride.

"You know, for someone who is so ... not tech-savvy, I can't believe your app worked," said Reed.

Dr. Patel chuckled. "I had nothing to do with the computer side. Only the science of compatibility. It worked because you and Sarai are two compatible spirits."

"Yeah." Reed felt a phantom tingle in his left

palm. "We share a lot of the same views. We like a lot of the same things. That will make for lots to talk about in this relationship."

"No, you misunderstand me," said Dr. Patel. "I mean in the core of your soul, where your wounds lie."

Reed's brows squished together. That was not what he expected the good doctor, the man about to perform his marriage rites, to say about him and his betrothed. Their wounds matched?

"You both see yourselves differently than the world sees you. Your perceptions affect your actions. Sarai had a tough time with modeling. There's a lot of rejection in that industry."

"I know," said Reed. "She told me."

"That's good." Dr. Patel pressed his lips together, as though he were trying to hold something inside. It was very unlike the man. He either spoke his mind directly or made his feelings clear as he bore into his patients. "But I'm fairly certain she hasn't told you everything."

Sarai had shared a lot with him. But Reed wasn't fooled enough to think there weren't some things they both held back. There may have still been secrets between them, but there was a lifetime for them to tell each other everything.

"I won't break patient-doctor confidentiality," said Dr. Patel. "I'll just tell you to accept yourself. But accept her, too."

Reed frowned, certain he was missing something. "I do accept her, just as she is."

"Good." Dr. Patel patted him on the shoulder. "Just be aware that she might not believe you when you tell her that."

"I think she believes I accept her. She is marrying me, after all."

"That's because Sarai is a smart girl," Patel smiled. "Don't let her hide who she truly is from you. And you don't hide either."

Reed wasn't one for trying to solve riddles. He liked hard truths and logical facts. His brain couldn't comprehend when Dr. Patel spoke philosophically.

This wasn't a conversation about facts. It was clearly one of those advice talks that a father would give his son before he walked down the aisle. Reed appreciated Dr. Patel for the gesture. But he was ready to get on with the main event.

"I don't see any faults now," he said. "But if and when I do, I'll keep my vows and the promises I'm ready to make to her."

Dr. Patel nodded. "Yes, I believe you will."

CHAPTER FOURTEEN

*Y*ears in modeling made certain that Sarai learned her best angles. She turned to the right and left in the mirror. She turned all the way to the back and looked over her shoulder. The angle didn't matter. She was a hot mess dressed in white.

When she'd been dress shopping with Maggie and Eva yesterday, they'd all had a fantastic time. Eva and Maggie were two bundles of joy that chattered and smiled and laughed and made Sarai feel as though she'd fit in for the first time in a long time.

On the drive into town, they'd regaled Sarai with their own shotgun marches down the aisle. Though each of their weddings was quickies, their marriages were both solid as rocks. And the two women were the happiest people Sarai had ever met. She wanted some of that, and it was possible with her and Reed.

The women had filled in more details about the ranch and the men, particularly Reed, over lunch. Maggie, the aspiring veterinarian, had had a turkey burger, while Eva, the college student, had had pasta. Sarai had picked at a salad, moving the leaves around her plate as she listened to stories of Reed and his antics with the other soldiers.

All too soon the women had gotten down to business. They pulled up at a wedding dress shop and the torture began.

Sarai hadn't looked directly in the mirror as she'd tried on the proffered dresses. She did not trust the store's glass after her encounter last week. So, she had decided to rely on the other women and their judgment.

Big mistake.

When Maggie and Eva's eyes had lit up at their first sight of the third dress, Sarai thought maybe she had a winner. Looking at herself in the mirror now, she saw nothing but disaster.

The dressed was ruche city. Ruching on the

bodice, ruching over the hips, ruching on the backside.

Every model knew that the art of ruching fabric was designed to hide the body's flaws. The gathering of the cloth was designed to flatter a less-than-flat tummy. It was laid out to loosen the roll of love handles. It was blocked out to bury a big backside. Each of Sarai's flaws was hidden behind the carefully crafted textile and everyone would see.

"You look so gorgeous."

Sarai turned as Maggie came into the room. How had she taken Maggie's kind and complimentary words for the truth? Sarai knew girls complimented each other but didn't really mean it. That behavior was rampant in the modeling industry. Girls would smile in each other's faces and, a second later, go behind the other's back to get a skinny leg up.

"She does, doesn't she?" Eva came up behind Sarai, placing her hand on Sarai's back. "I would kill for your hips. You look like Marilyn Monroe."

Maggie nodded in agreement. Both women gazed with wide eyes and wide grins at Sarai's form in the reflection. The forced smile on Sarai's lips was so brittle she was certain it would crack at any minute.

Marilyn Monroe had been a size sixteen in her life; size twelve by today's standards. That was not a compliment in high fashion where size six was considered plus size. Sarai hadn't let herself go that far—yet.

She was still clinging to a size eight. The wedding dress was a size nine. She hadn't looked when she'd tried it on. But she'd caught a glimpse of the tag today.

"Oh, sweetie, are you crying?" Maggie pulled a few tissues from her purse.

Before her new friend could wipe away Sarai's tears, Sarai grabbed the tissues from the other woman's hands. No way was she letting anyone near her carefully made-up face. Her dress might be a disaster, but her contouring was on point.

Sarai had khol'd her eyes and accented the sharp tips with a dusting of gold glitter. Her blush also had hints of gold glitter. The effect brought out the red of her Middle Eastern skin tone. She might be ashamed of her weight, but not her heritage. Not even on a ranch filled with US Army vets.

She'd expected a bit of animosity, but there hadn't been even a hint of it. Each man had welcomed her with a smile, a hug, or a peck on the cheek. The peck had come from Xavier Ramos, the soldier Reed had told her to watch out for. But the caution had been given with a quirk of the lip and a roll of the eyes, not a frowning glare.

Everyone on this ranch cared deeply for one another. Reed had told her stories about each person on the ranch in their chats. But seeing it in real life, seeing the support and the friendship and the care, it made Sarai ache at an emptiness somewhere other than her belly.

Maybe Maggie and Eva truly believed this crimply, concealing dress was pretty? Maybe their smiles were genuine? Misguided though they might be, Sarai didn't believe their compliments. Even though she wished they were true. The woman they spoke about and praised and said was beautiful, Sarai simply didn't see that woman reflected back in the mirror.

"Oh, Miss Sarai, you look like a real live princess." Rosalee's eyes were big and bright as she stared at Sarai's form. Eva's little sister was coming in the door, so she couldn't see Sarai's reflection in the mirror. What Rosalee saw was Sarai in the flesh.

One thing Sarai knew; kids didn't lie. They could be brutally honest little beasts, as she discovered in grade school. Sure, they could fib. But not when it came to compliments. Sarcasm was a learned skill that took years to master.

"When I get married," Rosalee continued, "I want to look just like you."

Sarai turned away from the mirror so that she met the little girl's gaze. Rosalee's brown eyes were open so wide with wonder that Sarai saw a reflection there. What Sarai saw reflected in the depths of Rosalee's eyes was someone she didn't recognize. The woman dressed in white was indeed beautiful. So much so that it took Sarai's breath away.

"It's time," said Maggie.

Rosalee turned toward the door and the vision was gone. The little girl pulled open the door, and Sarai was blinded by a bright light.

It was sunlight. That light encouraged her to leave her old life behind. It beckoned her on to a new life.

Sarai stepped out into the light. When she did, a sea of faces greeted her. Each of them was smiling. There wasn't a single sneer or smirk or pinched brow. Each face gazed at her in appreciation, in awe, in admiration.

Reed stood at the end of the walkway. He looked like something out of a catalog in his dark suit.

When he found her gaze, he clearly mouthed the words, *you're beautiful.*

Nothing made sense to Sarai any longer. And that was fine. The sun on her face warmed her. The breeze in the air cooled her skin. The steps she took were in the right direction.

CHAPTER FIFTEEN

*R*eed almost didn't recognize the woman that walked toward him. That must be a product of getting to know someone's personality first, seeing the beauty of who they are on the inside and coming to care for and respect that aspect of a person before they have a chance to present themselves physically.

He had already believed Sarai Austin to be a beautiful person. Her intelligence knocked him off his feet. Her wit took his breath away. Her sense of humor made the butterflies rise from his gut to his chest.

Even before he'd seen her, he'd known she was a beauty. Walking toward him, dressed all in white, with the sun shining down on her, she was positively breathtaking.

His legs buckled, and he reached out for something to hold onto. Luckily, Sean stood beside him and had his back. He caught Reed by the shoulders and gave each of his biceps a steadying squeeze until Reed could stand on his own two feet again.

It was just in time because Sarai, his bride, his wife to be, had arrived.

She reached out to him. Without thinking, Reed offered her his left arm as she came to stand on the left side of him. Sarai wrapped her fingers around his prosthetic forearm. Reed could have sworn he felt the heat of her fingertips on the flesh that was no longer there.

She smiled up at him. There was a look there, something he'd seen before in her eyes. Underneath the heavy kohl of her lids was a hint of doubt mixed with a tinge of fear. He'd seen it the first time they'd engaged the video chat feature.

Sarai was nervous. He'd rushed her back then to turn on the camera. Was he rushing her again?

Reed leaned down and whispered in Sarai's ear, "Are you sure?"

He felt the intake of her breath at the side of his

cheek. Had he called it correctly? Was she regretting the speed at which things were moving between them?

And then she sighed. It was the little exhale of breath that he knew so well from their audio-only chats. The sound that told him that she was not resigning. She wasn't one to give up easily. She was about to move in for the kill, and Reed couldn't wait to hear her rebuttal.

When he pulled away, she was smiling at him. The doubts and fear were gone. Trust and hope sparkled in her gaze. It was all the answer he needed.

He turned them both to face Dr. Patel in his role as pastor. The man eyed the couple with that small smile that said he knew more than he let on. Pastor Patel began the ceremony, and before Reed knew it he was reciting his vows.

Reed turned back to Sarai and repeated the words that Patel had prepared for each of them. With such a quick wedding, neither had a chance to write their own vows. But with both Reed and Sarai having a history with the man officiating their union, they trusted Patel to choose vows that suited them both.

"Sarai, I will love you no matter what. I will

always be honest with you, kind, patient and forgiving. I give you my hand and my heart as a sanctuary of warmth and peace. I pledge my love, devotion, faith, and honor as I join my life to yours. I take you to be my partner for life, promising above all else to live in truth with you and to communicate fully and fearlessly."

As vows went, these ones were spot on. With each word that left his lips, Reed felt the truth in them. Their relationship had begun with communication, honest discussions free of any physical distractions. It would continue that way as they set out as partners who lived fully and fearlessly.

"On this day," Reed continued to parrot the pastor with words that were spoken straight from his heart, "I give you my heart, my promise, that I will walk with you, hand in hand, wherever our journey leads us, living, learning, loving, together, forever. This is my sacred vow to you, my equal in all things."

A tear ran down Sarai's cheek. Reed lifted his right hand to brush the tear away. When he did, it left a smudge at her cheek rendering her makeup job imperfect. It didn't matter an iota to him. She still looked perfect.

"Reed," Sarai began her recitation of vows as

prepared by her former psychologist. "I will pay attention to your physical and emotional needs. I will grow with you, not apart from you. I will take care of my health so that I can be here with you as long as possible."

She stumbled over those last words. Her head dipped slightly. But only for a second. She inhaled and let out that sigh he knew so well.

"I will always show you with my words and my actions that I am yours alone forever. I take you to be my partner for life. I promise above all else to live in truth with you and to communicate fully and fearlessly. You are my true counterpart. I will love you, hold you and honor you. I will respect you, encourage you and cherish you in health and sickness, through sorrow and success, for all the days of my life. This is my sacred vow to you, my equal in all things."

Listening to the woman he would spend the rest of his life with making these solemn promises to him, Reed came to a realization he never thought his logical mind would deduce. It was entirely logical that a person you knew for a short time could become your entire world. Sarai was that for him now; his entire world. He would spend the rest of his days holding up to those promises he'd just made.

"You may now kiss the bride."

Reed's hands itched to take hold of her. He reached both out. Only to pull back his prosthetic.

Sarai wrapped her fingers around those fake digits. She stepped into him, lifting his left hand and placing her cheek in the palm of his fake hand.

Reed swore he felt the softness of her cheek in his phantom palm. He couldn't wait any longer. Some part of their duties as husband and wife would hold. But not this part. Not this taste of her. Not this moment where he would claim her as his own.

He pulled her to him, fitting her lush curves against his hard chest. It was just a press of the lips. A chaste kiss by any standards. But Sarai's lips were a starburst of joy. Her sweetness overwhelmed him, and he decided he would not ever let go.

At some point, their lips broke apart, but he did not relinquish his hold on her. At some point, they were announced as a new union, but he felt like they'd never been apart. At some point, they were pulled apart for congratulatory hugs, but she still felt connected to him.

Sarai was a part of him legally and spiritually. But she felt a part of him physically. Like his phantom limb brought back to life.

CHAPTER SIXTEEN

Sarai held tight to Reed's prosthetic hand. Her grip was so absolute that she was glad his fingers weren't flesh and bone, otherwise, she was sure she'd break them.

That kiss had nearly done her in. She'd been kissed before. Some of Europe's most practiced playboys had sought her out thirty pounds ago. They all paled in comparison to the heat of Reed's lips against hers. The warm, spicy gust of his breath as it brushed her cheek. The flutter of his lashes against her forehead. She was left lightheaded and dizzy in the face of a kiss that could run on daytime Disney.

She didn't let go of him when they paraded down from the gazebo to greet his friends as husband and wife. She held tight to him as he led her to the makeshift dance floor outside the barn. She kept her fingers laced around his forearm when they sat to eat, and he heaped food onto her plate.

The sight of the fried chicken and the smell of the barbecue sauce made her stomach churn and grumble at the same time. She was able to ignore those diverging feelings. But her heart fell into her gut when Reed held up his fork to her with a choice bit of meat.

"I couldn't eat a thing," she protested.

Reed lowered the fork with a frown. "I thought you loved chicken."

"I do. I'm just all nerves right now." Sarai took a deep breath. She let out a slow sigh as she prepared a better excuse for her unsatisfied appetite.

"But you have to smash the wedding cake in Uncle Reed's face," said Rosalee. The little girl was perched across from them on the other side of the table. Her plate was heaped with fried foods, barbecue sauce, and chips.

Down at the other end of the table, Sarai caught sight of the two-tiered cake that Dylan and Maggie had picked up from the local grocer. One of the first things Sarai had learned was that her new friend, Maggie, wasn't ever allowed near a kitchen. Just looking at the sugar-laden, calorie-packed, preservative rich cake made the buttons at her back strain.

To one side of the cake, Sarai caught Dr. Patel eyeing her. He said nothing with his mouth. He was busy helping himself to the barbecue and macaroni salad. But his eyes spoke volumes.

That's one thing Sarai didn't miss about therapy. The scrutiny.

Dr. Patel never put her down or judged her outwardly with harsh words. But his quiet, compassionate gaze that said *I care*, said it way too loud.

She didn't want Reed to hear that look. She didn't want any of these new people that were eager to be her family to see the judgment in Dr. Patel's eyes. Sarai's entire body tensed. Her fingers clutched Reed's.

He winced and twisted his hand inside hers. She was sitting at his right side now, and she was holding on to his flesh and bone.

"Sarai looks too beautiful to have cake smushed in her face," said Reed.

"Probably 'cause you want to kiss her face," said Carlos, Rosalee's older brother. No sooner had the words left the teenager's lips did he immediately turn red.

A chorus of manly chuckles and feminine giggles spread around the table. The dogs, who sat at everyone's feet, barked and yipped with glee.

The cake was handed out. There was inevitably a bit of smushing. Carlos smashed a piece in his sister's face. Rosalee ran after her brother threatening a sweet treat in retaliation. Sarai relaxed inside of Reed's embrace as she watched the cake move farther and farther away from her.

"How did I get so lucky?" he whispered in her ear.

She wanted to tell him that she was wondering the same thing. She couldn't remember ever being this happy. Not when she got her first modeling contract. Not when she took her first steps on a Parisian runway. Not when she booked her first magazine spread.

From the moment she walked to Reed at the altar, he hadn't let her go. He hadn't stopped telling her how beautiful she looked. And she was starting to believe him.

The afternoon turned to dusk, and she never left his arms. They sat and talked. They swayed on the dance floor. They stood and they laughed with others. Reed introduced her to all the dogs, including Soldier who danced between Sarai's heels. As she and her husband danced and laughed, Sarai forgot to feel self-conscious in her dress.

Soon, Sarai and Reed left their friends, the dogs, and the food behind as they walked the path to his house. Her new home. Her new life.

"I'm sorry no one from either of our families could be here," said Reed.

Sarai shrugged. "I'm excited to get to know the family that showed up."

The residents of the Bellflower Ranch, or as they preferred to call it, the Purple Heart Ranch, were all proving themselves to be a group of genuine individuals who truly cared for one another. And, over the last two days, it seemed they were open to bringing Sarai into their caring circle.

"They can be a handful." Reed's tone was ominous, but the smile on his face softened the blow.

"I don't mind."

"Famous last words." Reed chuckled.

Sarai felt the rumble of his laughter as it rolled through his body and straight to her heart. She'd heard him laugh many times during their talks. Watched it a couple times when they'd video chatted. Today, she'd felt it rush through her, over and over again as he sat next to her, held her in a loose embrace, and now walked beside her.

It was an addictive feeling. One that she planned to glut herself on. Unlike her relationship with food, this addiction wasn't one that could hurt her.

Reed would never hurt her. Of that, Sarai was sure. She just needed to make sure she didn't disappoint him.

"This is us," said Reed as they stopped in front of his door, their door.

Reed turned the knob. It was unlocked. There was no reason for it to be locked on a ranch where everyone was family.

Sarai looked down at the threshold. It was customary for the groom to carry the bride into their new home. She certainly hoped Reed wasn't thinking that. Not with her weight.

He reached out his arms as though he were going to attempt it.

Sarai stepped back. "Reed, don't you dare."

"I could," he looked defiant. "I could carry you in my arms. This thing is plenty sturdy." He held up his prosthetic.

Sarai tried to hide her grimace. It was the first direct mention he'd made of her weight. But as comments went, it wasn't the worst she'd ever heard.

"I am a big girl. I don't want you breaking your back over some silly tradition."

"Hey?" He chucked his finger under her chin, lifting her gaze to meet his. "I don't want you to ever feel you're settling for less because you married someone with only one good arm."

Again he held up his prosthetic, indicating that was the good arm. It did the trick. A bemused grin made its way onto Sarai's face.

"Sarai, I'm going to get everything I ever wanted because you married me."

They held for a moment. His finger under her chin. Her head tilted back. It was the perfect moment for a kiss. It was the logical thing to do in the circumstance. Her husband did not disappoint.

Reed tilted Sarai's head back a bit more. Then he leaned down and covered her lips with his. This kiss wouldn't make it past the Disney censors. Not when Reed's tongue slipped out to taste the top of Sarai's lip.

A warmth began in Sarai's gut. It was a powerful hunger. It pushed and shoved its way up her chest and into her throat. When Reed broke the kiss, her craving made itself known with a long, gluttonous sigh.

"Let's go inside," he whispered.

Sarai gulped. She continued to tremble. Not because of the cold air. Not because of the after-effects of the kiss. It was the anticipation of what happened next.

She was no virgin, but she hadn't been with a man in years. Certainly not while in her present condition.

But this was Reed, her husband. He couldn't back out of the relationship now that they were married. Not even when he saw her thunder thighs or her love handles or the flab at the backside of her arms.

"Today was amazing," he said, as he led her down the hall toward the bedroom.

"Yeah." At least she thought she said yeah. Her mind was fixed on problem-solving.

Perhaps she could convince him to keep the light off? Maybe she could feign modesty and ask him to leave the room while she changed? Then she could sneak under the covers and he'd be none the wiser.

"Wait?" They came to a halt, and she jerked back to the present. "This isn't your bedroom."

Reed's bedroom was across the hall. She knew because she'd peeked in there earlier this morning when she'd arrived.

"I know," he said.

"So ... we're ... you ...?" She didn't know what question she was trying to ask.

"This is technically our second date," Reed said. "I don't know about you, but I'm not that easy."

His response was so unexpected that Sarai blurted out a laugh. He was right. This was only the third day that they'd been together in real life. In her past dating life, even in the fast and loose lifestyle of a fashion model, Sarai had never slept with a guy after only a handful of dates.

"I told you," Reed said. "The plan is to meet you—check. Then to woo you—"

"Trust me, I'm wooed."

"I've already married you. I just need to check off courting you from the list. Can I take you out tomorrow, Mrs. Cannon?"

"Yes, Mr. Cannon."

"We may have rushed the marriage, but we're not going to rush the relationship building. We'll build a strong foundation. This is forever. So, we've got a bit of time."

And with a light peck at the corner of her mouth, Sarai's husband left her standing there hungry for more.

CHAPTER SEVENTEEN

*W*hy? Oh, why had Reed left his new wife at the spare bedroom door last night?

Because she'd been nervous through the ceremony and reception. Because she'd stiffened a couple of times while they were dancing when he'd pulled her close. Because she'd trembled when they'd crossed the threshold to their home, and he'd hinted at lifting her into his arms.

Dr. Patel's warning came to his mind as the new day's sun broke into his bedroom window. There was something about her that he didn't know, something she hadn't told him. Reed had no idea what that could be? He'd bared his soul to her. Didn't she trust him to tell him any and everything, no matter how dark?

Apparently not. But that was okay. For now.

He'd just have to work extra hard to make sure she knew there was nothing that would scare him away. He'd let her keep her secret for now. Whatever it was wasn't putting a wedge between them.

Reed didn't want anything coming between them. He wanted nothing more than to pull her closer. To hold her in his arms. To press his lips against hers.

Sarai had enjoyed the kiss that had turned them into an official union. She'd sighed into their second kiss as well. She'd been disappointed as much as she'd been nervous when she'd realized they wouldn't be sleeping together on their wedding night.

Reed knew consummation of a union was a requirement for marital legitimacy. It was necessary to sleep with one's spouse or face grounds for divorce. That didn't worry him. He had no doubt that this marriage would only be dissolved by death. He and his wife would only get physical once there was total trust between them and that included his wife telling him all of her secrets.

With that thought, Reed rolled out of bed. He left

off the prosthetic today as he dressed. There was no need to hide who he was. He'd lead by example for his family.

Reed opened his door at the exact same time that Sarai opened hers. She was dressed in track pants and a sweater. She looked lovely even though her curves were hidden.

The two newlyweds stared at one another. Then grinned. Then looked away.

"Hi," he said.

"Good morning," she said.

With the pleasantries out of the way, Reed didn't know what to do next? Should he go up and kiss his new wife? Should he only hug her? Should he keep his distance since this day, the first day of their marriage, would ostensibly be their third date?

They both took a step forward at the same time and nearly collided. So, they both took a step back. This waltz of uncertainty was getting them nowhere.

Finally, Sarai stepped up. She reached for his hand. Without thinking, Reed lifted the left one. Before he could pull his stump back, Sarai placed her hand on his flesh. Warmth flooded through his entire body. Until she jerked her hand away.

"I'm sorry," she said. "Is that okay?"

"Of course it is."

He offered his stump again, and she placed her hand gently on his mangled flesh. With his right hand, Reed pulled his wife into a hug. Sarai fit him so perfectly. There was nothing between them. In his mind, Reed began revisiting his courtship plan and its duration. For now, he planted a kiss at her temple.

"I was just about to make breakfast," Reed said.

"Oh. I'm not hungry. I'm not really a breakfast eater. Just gonna have some juice."

She twined her fingers with his. Reed pressed their palms together and felt that sense of deep connection that he'd felt when they'd said their vows. It was the most satisfying intimacy he'd ever experienced before in his life.

He regretted losing the connection as he opened the fridge. Sarai pulled the orange juice out of the fridge while Reed grabbed the eggs. She had her glass of juice in hand and was sipping her beverage while he was still assembling everything he needed.

"Can I help?" she asked.

"No, I've got it."

It took him longer to do simple things, like making an omelet. He never wanted his wife to doubt that he was capable of not only the simple domestic tasks but the larger ones as well.

He cracked the egg in one hand without any

shell spilling into the pan. He scrambled the eggs with the spatula. Placing the utensil down, he sprinkled on some cheese. Then picked up the spatula again to serve up his breakfast fare.

Joining Sarai at the breakfast nook next to the window, Reed asked, "So, what are we doing today, Mrs. Cannon?"

He would never get tired of the way she smiled shyly when he called her that. His wife shrugged in response as she sipped her juice. "Doesn't matter to me. I'm just happy to be here with you."

The only reason he didn't lean across the table to kiss his wife was that he had a mouthful of eggs. "Do you have to work?"

"No, I scheduled my posts for the next couple of days. What about you?"

"If I try to do any work around here this weekend, the guys will take my other arm."

She laughed at that. He loved that he could joke with her about his arm. It showed him that she truly didn't look down on his injury.

"Can we just stay in?" she said.

"I'm pretty sure that's what's expected."

Again she blushed. No, blushed was the wrong word. When her cheeks heated, Sarai glowed.

"We can veg out on the couch and watch the idiot tube," he suggested.

"That sounds lovely."

"I'll grab some snacks."

Reed placed his dishes in the sink. Then he turned to the cabinet filled with chips and sweets. Opening things could be a challenge for Reed, especially bags that required a two-handed grip. But he'd had gotten pretty good at using his teeth. He ripped the bag of chips and put them into a bowl.

When he presented his offering to Sarai she grimaced. "There's a lot of calories in that."

"Don't tell me you're still on a diet."

She squirmed as she curled her feet under her bottom at one corner of the couch.

Reed placed the bowl of chips on the coffee table and sat down in the center of the couch. "You should know I think you look perfect."

"I'm not perfect."

"Of course, no one's perfect. I was attracted to what was on the inside of you. And now that I see the outside ..."

He saw her breath catch. She held it instead of exhaling while she waited for his answer.

"Sarai, you're beautiful inside and out."

She swallowed but looked like she was having a tough time doing so.

Reed rose from the couch, taking the chips with him. He chucked the chips in the trash. Going back to the snack cabinet, he reached for a bag of popcorn. "Empty calories. Better?"

She smiled and nodded.

He came back to the couch with the approved snacks. Sarai had moved from the corner and now sat in the center. Reed shared the cushion with his wife. They sat in a companionable silence for nearly five minutes before Reed noticed that they stared at a black television screen.

"What do you want to watch?" he asked.

Sarai shrugged. Her shoulder bumped his, and he felt heat flare through him. He scooted closer until their shoulders touched. She didn't shy away from his arm.

"I have the complete *Star Trek* series on DVD starting with the original series," he offered.

"I've never seen the originals. I did watch a few of the Next Generation with Captain Picard."

Reed pulled away from his wife and squinted down at her. "Picard?"

Sarai leaned back as well. Her gaze flicked Reed

up and down in challenge. "What's wrong with
Picard?"

"He's not Shatner," Reed snorted.

"Shatner always reminded me of a dirty, old
grandpa." Sarai wrinkled her nose.

Reed's hand went to his heart. "How did I not
know this about you?"

"What? It's not a big deal. I'm more of a *Star Wars*
kinda girl than *Star Trek*."

Reed shuddered. "This marriage is doomed."

Sarai poked Reed in his chest. "Are we having
our first marital fight?"

"Yes, we are and it's a big one, and now it's gotten
violent." He caught her hand and laced their fingers
together.

"Why don't we go to neutral ground then. How
about something we both like?"

"We missed the latest episode of *Doctor Who*
yesterday since we were, you know, getting hitched."

"I've been dying to see that episode."

Reed let go of his wife's hand and reached for the
remote, then hesitated. "Wait, are you all caught up?
I figured you wouldn't have seen the last few
episodes since you were in France."

Sarai's body tensed beside him. "They actually

show them in Europe first. It is a British show after all."

"So, you've already seen the latest episode already?"

"No. I've been so busy."

"Too busy for the Doctor?"

"Maybe I was waiting for the right person to watch with."

The electric strings of the high pitched Theremin sounded through the television speakers. The familiar tune raced, keeping pace with Reed's heart. He stretched his stump and rested it on the back of the couch behind Sarai's head.

Sarai shifted.

Reed immediately lifted his arm, certain she was trying to get away from him. He was wrong.

His wife scooted her body closer to him. Then she rested her head and snuggled into the nook of his shoulder. Reed relaxed his arm. As the show droned on, he realized he'd need to watch it again. He was so intuned to his wife that he didn't hear anything after the opening music died away.

CHAPTER EIGHTEEN

Sarai woke the next morning. The grumbling of her stomach woke her before her alarm clock.

She'd spent the day with Reed watching *Doctor Who*, then movies, at some point she'd fallen asleep. She vaguely remembered Reed leading her to her bedroom. She clearly remembered the feel of his lips on her forehead.

She was so tired that she couldn't lift her arms to bring him under the covers with her because that was certainly her dream; staying in bed all day and night with her husband. But neither of them were ready for that. Sarai wasn't sure she'd ever be ready to be completely bare in front of her husband in body or soul.

He'd told her she was perfect to him. He'd called her beautiful inside and out. It wasn't the first time he'd said that to her. The more he said it the more she believed it just might be the truth.

Sarai wrapped a thick robe around herself, gathered her toiletries, and made her way to the shared bathroom at the end of the hall. Reed's door was shut and the living room was empty. He must be either still asleep or already out. She wasn't sure which as she didn't know her husband's schedule outside of their daily video chats.

Inside the bathroom, Sarai took a quick shower. The steam from the hot stream fogged the mirror, which was a good thing. She didn't need to see herself today. But as she patted her body dry the fog cleared. Sarai looked up into the mirror and caught a look at herself. Her reflection in the glass was hardly recognizable. She looked, not exactly thinner, but definitely different.

Was it possible? Had Reed's words changed her view of herself so much that it was manifesting physically? Her gaze dipped down away from the mirror to look at herself in the flesh.

There was still the cellulite on her inner thighs. But she had to stare before she could see the lines clearly. Her belly looked a little less like the top of a muffin, but there was not one single pack visible, let alone six. But there was a difference.

Then, looking down near the toilet, she saw it. A scale. It was a cheap store bought platform that was likely inaccurate.

Did she dare?

Sarai let the towel drop to the ground. Then she picked it back up making sure to wipe away every single drop of water that held onto her skin. Once dry, she hung the towel on its rack.

She closed her eyes and took a tentative step. Once balanced on the scale she still couldn't get her eyes to open. This was a bad idea. She did not need the disappointment today; the second day of her marriage to the man of her dreams.

She was going to step down. Her eyes opened so that she could see where she was stepping. Of course, her gaze fell on the needle of the scale. Sarai gasped at what it told her.

Five pounds? That couldn't be right. She stepped off the scale, then stepped back on again. It told the same story.

She was down five pounds.

Five. Whole. Pounds.

She wanted to dance. She wanted to shout. It was working.

Rosalee had said she looked like a princess. Eva and Maggie had said she'd looked pretty. The guys had all looked at her with appreciation, not leering like men did when she was a model. It was respectful.

And then there was Reed. Reed who thought she was beautiful inside and out. Reed who said she was perfect. She could be perfect. She just needed to stay the course she was on.

She was consuming foods. Just not solids. Only liquid. It had worked for her last photo shoot. It was working now. Just a few more days, maybe a week or two, and she would be even closer to her goal weight.

Sarai stepped off the scale and came back face to face with her reflection. It might be the steam but looking in the mirror it did look like her love handles were a bit flatter. She wondered if her arms were still flap-tastic. She lifted the left one slowly and—

"Sarai? You in there?"

Sarai dropped her arm with a *thwap*. She grabbed for the towel and flung it around her work in progress of a body. She might be improving but she was not ready for primetime, especially not in the daylight hours.

"I'm just finishing up," she called.

"Meet me in the kitchen when you're done, I'm making breakfast."

Sarai waited until she heard the sounds of her husband walking away from the bathroom door. Then she slipped out quickly and darted into her room.

The wardrobe she chose today was sure to flatter all her best parts and hide what still needed work. First thing was first, two layers of Spanx were a necessity. Over the Spanx, she pulled on her best jeans, the ones that molded her backside into an upside down heart. The shirt she chose was long sleeved to hide any possibility of flabby wings.

"Hey," Reed said looking up at her when she came out of her room. "Wow, you look beautiful."

Sarai took in a deep breath, but it didn't fill her lungs. The air only just made it down to her diaphragm which was constricted by all the spandex.

"I was thinking I could show you around the ranch today? Maybe you could help me with my chores?"

"Farm work?"

"You're a ranch wife now. You'll need to understand how things work here."

"Will this have anything to do with manure?"

"We won't muck out the stalls today, but you will need to put on a good pair of boots."

Sarai looked down at her silver boots. She pointed her steel-plated toe and lifted the heel. "These are Givenchy."

"Whatever they are, they won't make it back alive. You can put on a pair of running shoes for now. We'll head into town and get you a sturdy pair later."

"Fine." Sarai went back to her room and looked for a pair of sneakers that matched her outfit. She'd cleaned out her closet back at the house she and Mason had shared, but she still had a few storage units of clothing that were sample-sized. The best she could do was a pair of Gucci tennis shoes. But they were from two seasons ago. They were castoffs from Mason, so she didn't mind if they got scuffed.

"Morning fuel." Reed held up a glass of fresh squeezed orange juice to her when she came back into the room.

"Where'd this come from?" She'd seen how he'd had to maneuver yesterday as he'd prepared his breakfast and the snacks. Working with one arm proved more challenging than she'd imagined, but Reed handled it all in stride. She'd never heard him once complain or make a fuss.

"We have a juicer."

Sarai looked over to see a disassembled contraption in the sink. There wasn't an orange rind or gut to be found. Reed had made the drink and done the clean up all with only one arm and no assistance.

The sweet citrus of the fruit juice hit the back of her throat and raced down to fill her empty stomach. Sarai ignored the rumble of her stomach as she marveled at the abilities of this man she'd married. Again, she reaffirmed her vow to be the woman he deserved in body as well as in mind.

CHAPTER NINETEEN

*R*eed escorted his wife around the ranch on his arm. It was like they were back in a time of gentlemen and ladies. Soldier nipped at their heels as they walked.

Well, the Chihuahua nipped at Sarai's heels. The moment Reed and Sarai had stepped outside of the house, Soldier had taken one look at Sarai and offered his single front paw. Sarai had squatted down and accepted his paw and then a series of amorous licks. Soldier hadn't stopped gazing up at her since. Reed understood the sentiment.

Sarai wasn't dressed for the real chores he had to do this morning, and he'd assumed she wouldn't be up to his real duties just yet being that she was a former model and now a makeup blogger. So, he'd already gotten up and mucked out the horses' stalls earlier this morning. He'd saved the fun bits for her.

Reed watched Sarai's eyes light up as she fed the baby goats. The furry kids all crowded her as she held out food. As they passed by they left little presents all around the ground. Yep, those fancy, poor excuse for sneakers of hers weren't making it back into the closet. But she didn't seem to mind.

When the goats were fed, Reed took her to his favorite part of the ranch. His favorite chore. He took Sarai to the garden.

Reed loved the feel of the fresh soil in his hand. He loved working the earth, taking something from a seedling, feeding, watering and nurturing it until it grew into something tall and proud that he could then consume. Having Sarai work the earth with him was one of the most satisfying experiences in Reed's life.

But when he saw her perspiring and constantly dabbing at her head, he decided it was time for a break. He extended his arm to Sarai. As she came to her feet, she wobbled.

Reed pulled her close until she was steady. It felt good to have her body pressed against his. But concern for her health outweighed his desire for her.

"You okay?" he asked.

"Just stood up a little too quickly." Her eyes were closed, and she took deep breaths.

Reed held her to him. Mostly out of concern. But a huge part of him just loved that he could finally touch this woman in the flesh. She was his perfect match. Even if she wasn't a Trekkie. He had time to work on that minor discrepancy.

He had the woman of his dreams in his arms. And he never planned to let go. Sarai took a deep breath and opened her eyes.

Her gaze was foggy at first. Soon they sharpened on him. Reed saw vulnerability reflected back at him, and so he pulled her closer.

"Better?" he asked her.

"The best." She breathed out a sigh and offered him a smile.

And just because he could, Reed bent his head down and brushed his lips against his wife's. Sarai tasted of salt and oranges and his.

"Get a room," he heard Xavier call.

Reed was tempted to make a lewd gesture to let his friend know exactly what he thought of his interruption. But his hand was filled with something precious. So instead, he turned his wife in the opposite direction and walked away.

"Tell me more about your time as a model," said Reed, breaking the tranquility of the moment.

"Why would you want to hear about that?"

"Because you never talk about it much. And it's a part of your life. And I want to know everything about you."

"It was a rough time in my life. Sure, I got to dress up, wear pretty clothes, and travel to exotic places. But they don't treat you like you're a human being with feelings. You're just a mannequin for their clothes or accessories or makeup. They're allowed to say mean things about you and you're just supposed to take it. Not only that, you're supposed to do something to change the mean things they point out about you, or you won't have a job. There's a lot of rejection."

"Dr. Patel mentioned that."

Sarai stopped walking. "Were you and him talking about me?"

"No. Yes. Not in a bad way. We were discussing our vows. He gave me a bit of a fatherly talk."

They picked up walking again. The breeze that was constantly present during the morning had left and only the rays of the sun touched their faces. Sarai was quiet for a minute as they walked on. It felt like she was leaning a bit more into him as they walked. Which was fine by Reed. He wanted her to know that she could lean on him for any and everything for the rest of their lives.

"I went to him to deal with the rejections," she said after a long pause. "My parents made me. It was the best decision in their otherwise poor parenting. I think they only did it because they wanted me to get better so that I could come back to work."

"Did you get better?"

She shook her head. "I left modeling. That helped the most."

"So, why did you do it for so long?"

Sarai shrugged. "It helped pay my family's bills. My mom was a model. My dad too."

"Your father was a model?"

Sarai nodded. "Now he's a photographer, and my mom is a fashion show director. They travel a lot now. That's why they couldn't come to our wedding."

"There's still so much I don't know about you," said Reed. "I want you to know that you never have to hide from me. Not anything. I accept you no matter what."

A storm of emotions played across her beautiful face. Then she let out a small sigh. Though it was small, Reed knew it was the harbinger of something big.

"I had an eating disorder," she said.

Reed's expression remained patient and accepting. Her confession didn't surprise him. It was a common issue with models. But now his mind rewound back to this morning when she only had orange juice for breakfast. Then it rewound earlier to the previous day when she didn't touch a single snack he'd placed on the table. And even further back to their wedding day when she declined the cake.

"Do you have anorexia?" he asked.

"No, it's not that. I don't have bulimia either. It's hard to explain."

"Whatever it is, know that I accept you for who you are. It doesn't change my mind about you. I ... Sarai, I love you."

Reed was becoming addicted to her small gasps. She did it when he surprised her. She did it when she was about to make a point that would unravel his stance on an issue. She did it each time just before he kissed her. And now he saw that saying those three words would elicit the response he was coming to cherish. He'd be saying those words a lot for the rest of their lives.

Even with the gasp, a storm of emotions played

across Sarai's face. First the vulnerability. Then a flash of disbelief. Finally, a hint of acceptance.

Her eyes glistened. Her mouth opened. Reed braced himself to hear his words repeated back to him from her heart.

But before she could utter a single syllable, tires screeched up the driveway. Reed didn't recognize the fancy car. But he got the notion that Sarai did.

She squinted in the high noon sun. And when she pulled her hand away she gasped. But this was a big gasp.

"Mason?"

A man stepped out of the luxury car. At least Reed thought it was a man. The guy was tall and lanky, but with a muscular top build that slimmed into a small waist. He wore a pink silk shirt and purple leather pants. And ... was he wearing eye makeup?

"I tried to get here earlier Rai Rai," the man—Mason—said.

Mason held his arms open wide. Reed felt like he was in the crowd watching a seventies rock star prepare to perform. Instead of belting out a rock opera, Mason squealed as Sarai came into his arms.

"What are you doing here?" asked Sarai. "I thought you booked the McQueen show?"

"I told that queen I'd catch him on the flip side. I had to see my girl get married. But it looks like I missed it by two days. And this must be the man of the hour?"

"Reed, this is Mason Lee, my best friend, and former roommate. Mace, this is Reed Cannon, my husband."

"Charmed, darling," said Mason.

Reed extended his hand. Mason did the same. But instead of a shake, Mason wrapped his fingertips around Reed's and presented his knuckles.

Reed wondered if he was supposed to kiss the man's knuckles? If so, that wasn't happening. He considered himself socially progressive, but that was going a bit too far.

Reed dropped the man's hand and put his arm around his wife. "I'm sorry you missed the ceremony."

"Don't be, darling. I was there for the whole courtship."

Sarai had talked with Mason about Reed? Reed couldn't remember if she'd talked much about Mason, her best friend, with him. He thought he remembered hearing the name once or twice.

In fact, now that he thought about it, he did remember. Sarai had said she was in Paris helping her friend at a fashion show. This must be that friend.

"You're looking amazing," Mason said to Sarai. "Marriage definitely agrees with you. You definitely have brightened since I saw you last month."

"Last month?" said Reed. "Weren't you guys together in Paris a few days ago?"

CHAPTER TWENTY

*T*he heat had been beating down on her all day. From the moment Sarai got out of the shower and came through the steam, she'd started sweating. She was certain the goats would at some point ignore the food in her palms and reach up to lick the sweat off her brow. Or worse, start chewing at the fabric of her shirt and expose her flesh.

But she'd escaped all that. Reed didn't see her sweat or her fat or her imperfections. He'd nearly pushed the thoughts from her own mind as he constantly looked at her without judgment. As he looked at her with adoration. As he looked at her with only love reflected in his eyes.

She knew it was love because it was what she felt

for him. It was a feeling deep inside her. A feeling she'd been afraid to bring forth into the light of day. Until he unveiled his own feelings.

She'd been about to do the same when Mason pulled up. Now, she stood under the glaring sun with nowhere to hide. She couldn't hide her lies under fabric or with makeup. She was laid bare and exposed.

Sarai forced herself to look at Reed. He still looked at her with the same love shining through his eyes. There was only a small cloud of confusion there. Sarai lacked the strength to shove those wisps of doubt away with more lies.

"Sarai?" Reed asked. "What's he talking about?"

Sarai looked to Mason. Her BFF sighed but gave her a look that said he'd have her back in this lie. The look also said that he wouldn't like it, and she'd get an earful as soon as they were alone.

Mason had been there through her ups and downs in her modeling career. He'd been there right after she'd fallen down and out of the spotlight. He'd been there through her treatment and after.

Mason stood by her now. He said nothing. He waited for Sarai to speak.

Sarai opened her mouth but felt nauseous. She

closed her lips and tried again. All that came out was the truth.

"I wasn't in France."

She opened her eyes and watched as the light dimmed in Reed's gaze. Clouds grew. Her own vision of the truth went hazy. But she continued with the facts.

"I was here the whole time."

"Here?" said Reed. "In Montana?"

She nodded. Or she thought she did. The movement felt heavy.

"But you said you were in Paris." Reed stepped away from her. "You lied to me?"

Sarai felt entirely untethered as her husband removed his arm from her back. She could step over to Mason, and he'd support her. But she wanted to stand beside Reed.

"You lied to me," Reed repeated. Clearly, he was trying to work out the problem in his head and not coming to a solution. "Why would you do that?"

Reed looked to Mason.

"Is there something between you two?" he asked.

"No," Mason and Sarai both said at the same time.

"I don't play for your team, soldier," said Mason.

Reed looked back to Sarai. "You didn't want to meet me? Is it because ..." He held up his arm.

"No," she insisted. Why did he always bring things back to his disability? "It's not you, it's me. I didn't want you to see me like this."

Confusion still clouded Reed's face.

"Look at me," said Sarai. "Really look at me."

Mason sighed. Sarai ignored him. Her best friend never understood what it was like to be a female model. The pressure was ten times worse for the girls than the boys.

Reed just stared at her, still not seeing the truth that was clear to see in front of him.

"This isn't the real me," said Sarai. "I'm not who you believe I am under all these layers of clothes and makeup." Her makeup was melting off under the glare of the sun. The double Spanx was squeezing the life out of her.

"Who are you?" Reed asked.

Who was she? That was a good question. She could see that the answer was coming clearer to her husband with every second the sun glared down on her back.

What she saw reflected back in Reed's gaze was something she recognized. She saw her flabby, pathetic self in his eyes. Reed's gaze was darkening, shutting her out. His rejection was imminent. He was finally seeing her as she truly was.

What had she been thinking?

She knew what she'd been thinking. She'd believed the app. She'd believed the logic. She'd thought that she and Reed were compatible on a deeper level, a level past the physical. She'd been so starved for affection, and now she would be denied any of it from the one person she wanted it from.

Sarai's head was so full but so light at the same time. There was almost no more fight in her. Almost. With her last bit of energy, Sarai reached out to her husband.

Reed pulled his prosthetic arm away from her.

It was too late for her to pull back. She found herself falling forward into the empty space he'd left.

The world was going dark. She thought she heard Reed call out her name. But the last thing she remembered was hitting the ground hard. Then all was black.

CHAPTER TWENTY-ONE

Reed's world was spinning. The sun glared down on his back as he stared at this woman, his wife, as she stood before him with her lies exposed.

He'd given his heart to Sarai. He'd opened up and let her in. Not just into his mind and heart, he'd let her into his arms. And she'd lied to him.

He couldn't understand it. She'd been here the whole time in Montana?

What did she mean this wasn't the real her?

What layers?

He'd spent weeks peeling back her layers, getting to know the woman she was. He knew who she was.

Didn't he?

They were a 98% match. The math was on his side. But it didn't calculate the lies and omissions.

But here stood this best friend whom he didn't know much about. There was also the eating disorder she'd only just mentioned. And she'd been here the whole time?

"Who are you?" Reed asked.

Sarai sighed, but this sigh was filled with defeat. She reached for him. But he pulled away from her.

He'd offered her his arm. He'd laid his wounds bare. And she had lied to him. This wasn't the girl he fell for. Who was she?

Sarai kept coming forward. But she no longer had her feet under her. Her gaze was unfocused. Instead of the green of her eyes, he saw only the whites.

Her eyes had rolled back in her head. Her body had gone stiff. She was fainting. She was falling.

Reed sprang into action. But it was too late. He reached out to her, but she slipped down his stump and through his hand. His fingers caught the edge of her shirt, but it wasn't enough of a hold, and she hit the ground.

Reed dropped to his knees beside her. He checked her pulse. It was there but shaky. He checked her breathing. She was still getting air. But she was unresponsive.

"We have to get her to Dr. Patel."

Reed put his hand under his wife. He gathered her back to him, but without a second hand, he couldn't lift her.

He looked to her friend Mason who stood paralyzed in shock. For all his muscles and build he didn't look like he could actually lift a woman.

Reed called out to Sean and Xavier. Within seconds, the two came running. Xavier lifted his wife effortlessly and carried her to the doctor while Reed trailed beside them uselessly. He'd vowed he'd be there for her. The first moment of crisis and he'd failed her.

Once inside Dr. Patel's office, they laid Sarai on the therapy couch. Dr. Patel set about examining her. He was patient. There was no sense of urgency. Reed paced the length of the floor, running the carpet ragged.

"When was her last meal?" Dr. Patel asked.

"Breakfast," said Reed.

"What did she have?"

"Orange juice."

"And? Is that all? What about dinner?"

Reed told the doctor the food diary he'd

cataloged moments before she fainted. Dr. Patel nodded as he listened to the sparse list. Then he looked past Reed as though he'd find more answers over his shoulder. Reed turned to see Sarai's best friend.

"She'd been doing good, doc," said Mason. "She hadn't had a relapse in almost a year. I've been out of town for a few weeks. But we talked every couple of days on the phone."

So had Reed and Sarai. But she hadn't told him about this issue. What else hadn't she told him?

"Did she tell you she has an eating disorder?" Dr. Patel asked Reed.

"She just did. Just a few minutes ago. But she's a healthy weight."

Reed looked down at his wife's body. She was curved in all the right places that a woman should be in just the way that would drive a man wild. Her shirt had ridden up over her midriff. Instead of flesh Reed saw black spandex. No, actually there was one blue layer of spandex covered by a black outer layer.

Was that a body shaper? Why would she think to wear something like that? And out in this heat?

Reed had no clue about women's sizes, but he knew Sarai was nowhere near what could be considered overweight or plus sized. Her waist was slim and he could see that her covered abdomen was concave beneath all the layers she wore.

She'd begun to tell him she had an eating disorder. That it wasn't the ones he knew about. What was this eating disorder?

"It's called body dysmorphia," said Dr. Patel. "She doesn't see her body the way others do. She sees imperfections where there may be none. She'll try to control her intake of food or work out excessively to achieve an unrealistic ideal."

Reed had thought he knew her so well. How had he not known this? How had he not seen the signs?

"I'm going to get some fluids in her and then have a chat," said Dr. Patel. "Why don't you give us some space?"

But Reed didn't want to leave her side. He'd already let her slip through his fingers once. He had to be here when she woke up so that she knew he was still by her side.

"I'll come and get you when she's ready," Dr. Patel assured him.

Reed stepped out the door. But he didn't leave. He intended to wait until his wife woke up.

CHAPTER TWENTY-TWO

*D*arkness surrounded her. Sarai saw nothing, not even a pinprick of light. But she was conscious and aware.

Her body ached all over, but mainly on the left side. The skin on her shoulder stung as she shifted and the material of her shirt rubbed against the torn skin. Her jaw ached when she winced from the pain of her shoulder. Her hip throbbed when she tried to curl into the fetal position seeking comfort from the pain.

She'd hit rock bottom again. Literally this time. But the pain didn't only radiate from her skin and bones. It went deeper. She felt it in her gut. Sarai was desperately hungry.

It went beyond her stomach needing food. Her

soul felt starved. Her spirit felt famished. Her heartfelt ravenous. Only one thing would satisfy her.

"Can I see her?"

Reed.

His voice broke through the darkness like a lightsaber coming to life. Her first instinct was to shield herself. To cover up the imperfections that ran rampant all over her body.

Her first thought was to check her makeup. What was she wearing? How did she look?

"I need her to know I'm here."

Sarai forced her eyes open. She didn't think she could feel any worse. But coming to and seeing that she was alone in an empty room did the trick.

Reed wasn't there with her. She was alone. But he was near, she could hear him. He was just beyond the door.

She tried to lift her head but it stung. She tried to move her arms but they felt leaden. She knew she wasn't trapped, that nothing held her down. But her body refused to do what her mind demanded.

Wasn't that irony.

Her illness caused her mind to play tricks on what she saw of her body. Her dysmorphia had driven her from her career, from her life, from her friends, from the man she loved. It had made her

believe that she'd gained too much, and so she'd
endeavored to lose what she could. Now her mind
wanted to reach out and claim what she'd lost. But
her body, her flesh and blood, was too banged up
and bruised to cause any change.

"I didn't catch her when she fell," said Reed. "She
needs to know I'm here for her."

The pain in her husband's voice caused Sarai to
whimper in pain. Her fall had left real bruises on her
body. A fall that happened because she'd slipped
back into old and dangerous habits.

Her illness had only ever caused her harm. Now
it was hurting the man she loved. Reed deserved
better.

"I just need her to know that I love her."

Sarai did know that. Despite every ill-conceived
perception in her mind, that one truth she believed.
Because she believed in Reed. He'd never lied to
her. He only told her the truth. He was telling
it now.

He deserved the truth from her. He needed to
know that they couldn't be together with the way she
was now. She was not well. She needed to be better.

The door opened. For the first time in a long
time, Sarai didn't scramble to cover her body. She
didn't try to shield her unmade face. It was painful,

but she was determined to face the truth. Instead of Reed's face, she saw Dr. Patel.

"You're awake," he sounded surprised. "How are you feeling?"

"Awful. Inside and out. I need help."

"Good. Your husband is outside. Would you like me to get him for you?"

"I don't want to see him right now. Not like this. Not yet."

She had one more makeover to do. This one, hopefully, would be her last one.

CHAPTER TWENTY-THREE

*R*eed popped up from a dark dream. Sarai fell through his arms again and again. Every time he closed his eyes to sleep, it happened again. And again. She slipped through his grasp.

He woke up with his heartbeat racing. His mouth was dry. His throat was sore as though he'd cried out in real life.

Reed scratched at the tightness in his chest. He knew he wasn't going back to sleep again. Adrenaline rushed through him. He had to do something. There was only one thing he wanted to do.

The sun was blinking a few rays of its light over the horizon. Reed rolled out of bed. There was no need for him to dress as he'd never taken off his clothes from yesterday.

Unclean, unshaven, and unkempt he marched over to the medical suite on the ranch. Dr. Patel had insisted that Sarai spend the night there in the small clinic for observation. Patel and his daughter, Ruhi, had taken turns watching over her through the night.

Sarai hadn't wanted to see Reed when she came to. That had gutted Reed. It was the hardest, most jagged pill to swallow. Dr. Patel had told him to give it a day, to give her the time she needed to work out a few things.

It was a new day. Time was up. She was his wife. They should face all their problems together.

As Reed pulled the door of the suite open, he saw both Patels speaking quietly in the corner. Their backs were to Sarai's door. Reed crept in with the stealth he'd learned in combat zones. He should've known he was no match for Dr. Patel.

The man's gaze lifted as his daughter flipped through paperwork. Patel glanced at Reed. His face was expressionless. When his daughter handed him the clipboard of papers, Dr. Patel's gaze went to it.

Reed took that as a green light. He turned the knob of Sarai's door and slipped in. Belatedly, he thought he should've knocked. But he knew there was no way he wasn't going inside.

He'd endured chats over the computer, calls over the phone, the barrier of a video camera. No more. His relationship with his wife would only ever from this day forward exist in reality.

Inside, Sarai slept peacefully. She was beautiful even in her sleep. Whatever her treatment would be to combat this illness would not involve them being apart.

Reed sat down on the twin mattress. He reached out his hand and brushed a sliver of hair from her face. There was a slight abrasion there, likely from her fall, and she winced.

"Reed?" Her eyes blinked open. She stared at him for a second, her gaze coming into focus, and then she started. "I'm not wearing anything."

She was fully clothed in pajamas. A sheet covered her midsection. But she didn't reach for the sheet. She covered her face with her hands. Just as soon as she covered her face, she pulled her hands away.

"I'm sorry," she said. "It's really hard for me to be exposed. Dr. Patel diagnosed me with body dysmorphia. It means I don't see myself-"

"The way that others see you," he finished for her.

"Yeah."

"How can I make you believe that I think you're beautiful?"

Sarai looked into his gaze. There was turmoil in her green eyes. "I don't know?"

"This is what Patel told me on our wedding day; that we needed to see each other as we are. And not let the other hide. You accept me for who I am?"

He lifted his stump and brushed the side of her face that wasn't bruised.

"I do," she said, leaning into his touch. "I do accept you, wounds and all."

"I accept you for who you are. We'll need to help each other out with our own perceptions."

Sarai hesitated but she didn't pull away from his embrace. "I love you, but I don't love myself. I don't think we can be together until I learn to."

Reed pulled her to him with this right hand, locking her into his embrace. "I'm not letting you go. I'll close my eyes and not look at you if that's what you need. But I am not letting you slip through my hands."

She turned her face into his chest. Reed felt the wetness of tears permeate his shirt.

"Sarai, I want you to look at me so you know the truth. I want you to see the proof."

She lifted her teary-eyed gaze to him. She didn't wipe away the tears. She let him see her raw emotion. It was a start.

"I got angry and confused yesterday," he said.

"Because I lied to you?"

"No. Yes." He took a breath and began again. "Yes, when I learned that you'd lied, that felt awful. I'd opened myself up to you, only to learn that you'd closed a part of yourself off from me."

"I won't lie again, I promise."

"I believe you. And when I learned more about your illness, after talking with Dr. Patel and Mason, I came to understand why. I spent the night studying it. The first thing I did was to take all the mirrors and the scale out of our home."

Reed ran his fingers around the abrasion on her cheek. Sarai closed her eyes as he did so. The sigh wasn't one of resignation. He knew then that she wasn't giving up on them. She was ready to fight.

"I can wait to share a bed with you. But you can't keep yourself from me, Sarai. You can't not talk to me. You are my addiction. I need you in my life. For better or worse, that was the deal. Sickness and health."

He pressed a kiss to her wounded flesh. Only a light kiss. But he needed his wife to know that he loved her despite any real or imagined flaws she might have.

"Please believe that I love you despite your wounds," he said.

"I do. I know that one thing is true. It's everything else I have a hard time trusting."

Sarai tilted up her head and met Reed's gaze full on. Her gaze was open, vulnerable. But at the edges of her green eyes, Reed saw certainty.

"I'm going to get treatment," she said.

Reed winced. "Is it inpatient?"

"Since Dr. Patel is here, I can see him on the ranch."

Reed sighed in relief. "I can wait for anything so long as I get to hear your voice, see your face, hold you in my arms. I swear, I will never let you fall again."

"I'm going to work hard to love me too."

"I believe you'll do it. Once you see how amazing you are. Just keep looking into my eyes. Trust the reflection you see there."

Sarai gazed into Reed's eyes. Her lids narrowed as she focused on the reflection in his gaze. After a moment, a small smile tugged at her lips.

Reed leaned down and captured her lips. He drank in that smile and tasted acceptance. He tasted love. He tasted commitment.

With one final brush of his lips against hers, Reed tasted who Sarai truly was. As he pulled away, he left behind his true essence. When he looked into her eyes he saw reflected who they would become together.

*I*t was another day in paradise. Sean Jeffries held up his hand, shielding his face from the sun. Up in a tree, a male bird sang a song to a female perched on at the edge of a branch. His notes were strong and pure, but Sean noticed a couple places on its wing where it looked like it had been pecked and a few feathers pulled loose.

Still, its song was intriguing enough for even Sean to hold still. With each note, he hopped closer and closer to his chosen mate. At the last note of the song, another male with bright, unmarred feathers swooped in. His song was a squawk, but his bird-body was perfect. He stole away the ladybird and they flew off together, leaving the wounded songbird alone and defeated.

Sean wasn't surprised. He knew that outward appearances mattered more than what was on the inside. The last year had taught him that truth which contradicted all the self-help books he'd read and seminars he'd attended in his life.

He lifted his hand and knocked on the door he stood in front of. He was sure to turn to his left side, placing his scars in the shadow as he did. He had no song to sing to this lady, but neither did he want to spoil her morning with his ruffled features.

"Good morning, Sean," Sarai said as she pulled open the door to the home she shared with her husband. "Reed's not here. He went out to help the others a couple of hours ago."

"I know. He sent me to take you to your appointment." Sean stepped aside and indicated the golf cart they sometimes used to get around the ranch.

Most of the men preferred to ride horses to their destinations on the property, but he knew that Sarai lacked the confidence to ride. She thought she was too big to fit on a horse. It was an unfounded idea. The woman weighed far less than Sean who rode for hours with no problem. But Sarai was still working on her body issues. With the help of her husband

and everyone on the ranch, she was making progress.

"Really?" Sarai cocked a hand on her hip. "He sent you to drive me less than halfway across the property?"

Sean shrugged. He would've done the same had Sarai beeches wife. The men on the ranch treated their wives like the precious treasures they were. And there was the fact that Sarai had collapsed in the heat shortly after her wedding. They weren't taking any chances with her health.

Sean handed her into the golf cart and they took off across the ranch. He would never tire of the beauty of this place from the rolling hills in the distance to the green pastures that stretched as far as the eye could see. But he would have to give it up soon.

"It's just a few weeks until the zoning deadline," said Sarai. "Are you headed down the aisle soon?"

"No. I don't have any prospects for matrimony."

"I find that hard to believe. A smart and handsome guy like you? Girls must be lined up at the gates."

They weren't. Sean rarely left out of the gates of the property. On the ranch, he didn't get constant stares at his scars.

"Have you tried online?" asked Sarai. "Reed and I were a ninety-eight percent match, you know."

Sean knew. But he also knew he wouldn't find the perfect match online, like Reed. Or bump into her at church, like Fran. Or have her fall into his lap, like Dylan. Those routes were closed to him.

As they pulled up to the medical suite, a small, energy efficient car that was just a touch bigger than the cart pulled up too. Ruhi Patel stepped out. When she did, Sean swore that the sun narrowed its rays on her casting her in a golden glow. The birds joined in chorus to sing the sweetest song ever heard. Flowers spontaneously bloomed as her feet touched the earth.

"Good morning, Sarai. You're looking healthy today."

"Good morning, Nurse Patel," said Sarai. "I love that shade of eyeshadow on you."

Eyeshadow? Sean hadn't noticed the artificial coloring just under Ruhi's brow. He'd always assumed it was her natural, inner glow.

"Sean. Sean?"

Oh no. She'd been speaking to him and he hadn't responded. He knew he hadn't been caught staring. He'd perfected his peripheral vision so that he would appear to be looking away from someone, but in truth, he'd be free to take in an eyeful. Sean always practiced that tactic when Ruhi was around.

He lifted his gaze to find Ruhi looking directly into his eyes. She was smiling at him. That smile often caught him off guard. So much so that his lips cracked a grin, a rare occurrence with him because when he did it further increased the grooves in his right cheek.

Ruhi's gaze slid to his scars and she cocked her head to the side. Sean didn't shy away from her perusal. Ruhi was the only person he held still for. She didn't pretend she didn't see his wound. She stared openly, challenging it to defy her healing prowess.

"I thought we weren't seeing you until tomorrow?" she said. "You doing okay?"

Ruhi lifted her hand to his face. Her index finger caught Sean's chin and she tilted his head so that she could get a better look at his wound. He allowed it. He shied away from everyone but her. She was the only good thing that came out of this cursed scar.

"Just dropped off Sarai for Reed."

Ruhi rolled her eyes but didn't let his chin go as she examined him. "The machismo on this ranch is so thick you could cut it with a butter knife."

Like Sean, Ruhi had come from a traditional

family with traditional values. Sean had gone through a rebellious phase as a teenager, but it hadn't lasted long. He ached for a wife to call his own, and children to run after, and a home to look after.

Ruhi was still rebelling against her upbringing. If it was a valued tradition, she turned the other way. As she turned to go into the building, a packet of papers fell out of her purse.

Sean bent to pick up the documents. His gaze settled on bold words; Doctors Without Borders. Sean knew of the program. It placed doctors in faraway places to help those in need. The documents were filled out in pen with Ruhi's slanted scrawl.

"You're leaving?" As the words left his mouth, Sean felt his throat closing.

"If I get in." She took the pages from him and placed them back in her bag. "This is the last stage of the application process. I'm on a short list now. I'd get to travel the world and help those most in need. It's a dream come true. Wish me luck."

Sean clenched his jaw. He watched her walk into the medical suite beside Sarai. The two women chatted away as they disappeared down the hall.

Sean's heart thudded and then it stopped

beating. He hadn't planned on getting married, which would've meant he'd have to leave the ranch. But he'd planned to stick around. If Ruhi left the ranch, there would be no reason for him to do even that.

A cloud moved in front of the sun. In unison, the flock of birds that had gathered at Ruhi's arrival took off into the air. Sean turned his scarred face back into the shadows and took off into the gloomy day.

That's only the beginning!
You know a romance novel guarantees an HEA.
Can't wait to find out how Sean and Ruhi get theirs?
The story continues in
His Permanent Scar
Book Four in the Brides of Purple Heart Ranch series!

Shanae Johnson was raised by Saturday Morning cartoons and After School Specials. She still doesn't understand why there isn't a life lesson that ties the issues of the day together just before bedtime. While she's still waiting for the meaning of it all, she writes stories to try and figure it all out. Her books are wholesome and sweet, but her are heroes are hot and heroines are full of sass!

And by the way, the E elongates the A. So it's pronounced Shan-aaaaaaaa. Perfect for a hero to call out across the moors, or up to a balcony, or to blare outside her window on a boombox. If you hear him calling her name, please send him her way!

You can sign up for Shanae's Reader Group at http://bit.ly/ShanaeJohnsonReaders

Also By Shanae Johnson

The Brides of Purple Heart

On His Bended Knee

Hand Over His Heart

Offering His Arm

His Permanent Scar

Having His Back

In Over His Head

Always On His Mind

Every Step He Takes

In His Good Hands

Light Up His Life

Strength to Stand

The Rangers of Purple Heart

The Rancher takes his Convenient Bride

The Rancher takes his Best Friend's Sister

The Rancher takes his Runaway Bride

The Rancher takes his Star Crossed Love

The Rancher takes his Love at First Sight

The Rancher takes his Last Chance at Love

The Rebel Royals series

The King and the Kindergarten Teacher

The Prince and the Pie Maker

The Duke and the DJ

The Marquis and the Magician's Assistant

The Princess and the Principal